Death
and the

Language
of
Happiness

ALSO BY JOHN STRALEY

The Woman Who Married a Bear
The Curious Eat Themselves
The Music of What Happens

Death
and the

Language
of
Happiness

John Straley

BANTAM BOOKS
New York • Toronto • London • Sydney • Auckland

DEATH AND THE LANGUAGE OF HAPPINESS
A Bantam Book / May 1997

Epigraph from "Trista." Reprinted by permission of Scribner, a Division of Simon & Schuster, from *Osip Mandelstam: Selected Poems*, translated by Clarence Brown and W. S. Merwin. Copyright ©1973 by Clarence Brown and W. S. Merwin.

Library of Congress Cataloging-in-Publication Data

Straley, John, 1953–
Death and the language of happiness / by John Straley.
p.   cm.
ISBN 0-553-09679-6
I. Title.
PS3569.T687D43   1997
813'.54—dc20   96-32610
CIP

Published simultaneously in the United States and Canada

Bantam Books are published by Bantam Books, a division of Bantam Doubleday Dell Publishing Group, Inc. Its trademark, consisting of the words "Bantam Books" and the portrayal of a rooster, is Registered in U.S. Patent and Trademark Office and in other countries. Marca Registrada. Bantam Books, 1540 Broadway, New York, New York 10036.

PRINTED IN THE UNITED STATES OF AMERICA
BVG   10 9 8 7 6 5 4 3 2 1

For Jan Morrison Straley,
who taught me to write

o indigence at the root of our lives,
how poor is the language of happiness!
Everything's happened before and will happen again,
but still the moment of each meeting is sweet.

OSIP MANDELSTAM

Death
and the

Language
of
Happiness

Chapter One

Sitka, Alaska—May

William Flynn had been a fine gardener by Alaskan standards and some people maintained he had also been a terrorist. All I know for certain is he raised a garden in tough country and he loved flowers the way other men love beautiful women. This story is about how William Flynn both was, and was not, responsible for the murders of two young people almost eighty years apart.

Like most things in southeastern Alaska, the story begins in the rain. The drops were falling hard as coins on an aluminum travel trailer parked under the mountain ash tree. The red berries from the tree had long ago bled into black pulp on the thick mâché of matted leaves. New grass sprouted in the disturbed ground. There was an abandoned pickup truck sinking into the spring mud next to the trailer, and a raven on the handlebars of a spilled red bicycle.

I could put most of it together from the reports. She had walked from the trailer to the liquor store and there had asked to borrow cleaning buckets and brushes. She drank deeply from the plastic liter of vodka. Then she rented a room in the cheapest hotel and washed the tub.

She scrubbed the porcelain and the grout, the fixtures and the tile above the bath. She spent perhaps two hours doing it, as carefully as if she were trying to polish one white pearl out of the world dark as coal. Then she took off her clothes and laid them neatly on a plastic bag and put the .22 pistol on the closed toilet lid.

She let the water run a long time, clearing it of any trace of rust, then lowered herself into the tub slowly, her lean body creating and filling the hole in this tiny artificial lake. Her black hair floated like a kelp bed and her breasts lifted free, the redness of her brassiere still etched on her skin.

She scrubbed her bruised and calloused knuckles. She washed her hair. She gripped an orange stick in her shaking hands, pushing the cuticles back from the half moons of her fingernails. She used cotton swabs and alcohol to clean the pink folds of her ears and around the creases near her eyes and nose.

When the young policeman knocked on the door he called out that her children had been badly beaten. But there was only the sound of running water on the other side of the door. When the policeman opened it with his weapon drawn he saw the young woman's face pulled out of shape like a sagging rubber mask. The back of her skull had been blown out by the exit wound from a large-caliber slug. The bath water was running across the floor, the loaded and unfired .22 pistol was lying on the tile under the toilet.

The young cop vomited in the corner near the old radiator as the tub continued to overflow. The foamy water ran across the tile and over the doorjamb. Eventually the salesman in the room below called down to the desk, alarmed that blood was dripping from the light fixture in his ceiling.

Later the police found the gun used to kill the young woman in William Flynn's room in the retirement home.

They questioned Flynn about Angela Ramirez's murder but didn't hold him. I don't suppose they were too worried about losing him, thinking, as most people would, that a ninety-seven-year-old man couldn't run very fast, or far. The DAs would have time to poke around and make their charging decisions later.

I was organizing a birthday party for my roommate when both my lawyer and my psychiatrist called.

"Hey, Cecil, are you busy?" Dickie Stein's voice echoed over the line as if he were in the bottom of a well.

"Take me off that goddamn speaker phone, will ya?" I yelled at him as I kept stretching a skinny blue balloon.

"Sorry, man, but this is business. I'm here with Dr. Trout. You know the good doctor, I believe?" Dickie had on his adult voice.

"The pill man," I said and held the balloon to my lips.

"Cecil, how you doing?" I heard the doctor's professionally calming voice above the rustling of paper.

I took the balloon out from between my lips. "Do you mean 'How you doing?' like am I witnessing alien abductions? Or do you mean 'How am I doing?' "

"Start wherever you like. But don't work too hard on your story. I won't prescribe you any more drugs."

"Damn the bad luck." I stretched the blue balloon, trying to loosen its skin. My memory lingered on the comical little buzz I used to get by abusing the tranquilizers Dr. Trout prescribed. I cradled the receiver on my shoulder and kept talking. "Basically I'm fine. Other than the fact that I'm nearly indigent and I find sobriety to be a tedious bore."

"Glad to hear it," my shrink chirped.

"Hey, I need the services of a private investigator, Cecil." Dickie's voice cut in out of nowhere. "Are you free?"

"Just let me look at my calendar," I said and tried unsuccessfully to blow up the party balloon. My face turned red, my eyes hurt, and the balloon was still a rigid blue spike. I spoke back into the phone. "I'm completely yours. What do you have?"

"It's going to be a murder case." He paused and I could hear a sheaf of papers fall off his desk. Dickie generally believed in a composting style of office management. "You know William Flynn. Right?"

My stomach tightened. I knew William Flynn. I was in my forties but William Flynn had always been an old man, as far as I knew. He had lived with his brother in a remote anchorage to the southwest of Glacier Bay. William and his brother Tommy were fishermen and hunters who rarely made it to town. They were eccentrics of the cranky and opinionated sort you run into all over the North. I didn't know the Flynn brothers well, but had anchored in their cove one entire commercial fishing season the year I was trying to earn my college tuition. They were strange seditionists, as I remember. William would lure me to shore with hot meals and books from eastern Europe and Asia while Tommy would blister me with his opinions about the abuses of the ruling class. Tommy was gone now. I didn't remember when he had died, only that William turned up on the streets of Sitka sometime in the eighties and I would run into him walking through the gardens of the Pioneers' Retirement Home nodding and inspecting the flowers as if he were a collector at a rare art sale.

"Yeah. I know William Flynn," I told my lawyer.

Dickie's voice faded in and out. I imagined him picking up the file from the floor where I could also imagine the pizza box and the moldy cartons from Chinese take-out.

"Okay," Dickie blurted and his voice settled back into focus. "You probably know this stuff, Cecil, but I'll cover it all so we will all be reading off the same sheet of music." Dickie was at his most irritating when he tried acting like a real lawyer. It was just one of the ways that Harvard Law School had scarred him.

"Angela Ramirez is shot to death by a thirty-eight-caliber handgun while in the hotel bathtub. The police respond. Witnesses see William Flynn walking unsteadily across the street back toward the Pioneers' Home where he lives. The police find an antique thirty-eight-caliber revolver that appears to have been recently fired. The gun's been sent out for tests. The old man makes statements. Garbled stuff. He says Angela was going to leave him and he couldn't stand it. He says something about castration. I can't make much sense of it but he acts like he is covering for his brother Tommy, but as you know Tommy's been dead some eight years now. It's real nutty stuff, Cecil. But that's okay because Flynn's statement is suppressible."

"That's the good news? What do you need from me?"

"Well, Cecil . . ." my psychiatrist's voice came cutting through, "Dickie has asked me to evaluate Mr. Flynn's competency to stand trial. And I've been doing just that . . ." There was a pause in the line; no papers rattled.

"So, is he nuts or not?" I asked as I reached for a pink balloon.

"Let me get back to that . . ." My doctor was almost whispering now. "William is ninety-seven years old. He can walk short distances, but uses a wheelchair in the home. It's my understanding the DAs won't go to the trouble of charging him if he is not competent. It's a complex case so I'm going to keep my opinion to myself as long as the investigation continues, and as long as William Flynn remains a suspect."

"Okay . . . Again, what do you need from me?" I asked, beginning to feel a little jacked around by the professionals.

"Well . . ." he drawled out, "Mr. Flynn wants you to kill someone." The doctor's voice said it calmly.

"Really?" I stopped stretching the pink balloon.

"Actually, yes." He was speaking softly now so I could barely make out his words. "And the funny thing . . . Oh, not funny really . . . but the interesting thing is I think it could possibly help his legal situation. I know that sounds absurd—"

"What do you think, Dickie?" I cut Dr. Trout off before he sank deeper into his moral qualms. There would be enough time for those once we both started billing hours on the case.

"It's wacky stuff, Cecil," Dickie said. "But old Flynn seems to be talking about a possible witness to Angela Ramirez's killing."

"And the fact that he wants me to murder a witness to this woman's killing is good news? Isn't that a little optimistic?"

"Just go down and talk to Flynn, Cecil. Get a line on this guy. You have personal experience with this stuff." Dickie sounded happy.

"Which—insanity or tampering with a witness?" I tried the balloon again and my sinuses felt as if they were tearing.

"Both," Dickie said. "Just meet the doc down at the home and talk to Mr. Flynn, okay?"

"Give me a couple of minutes to blow up this balloon," I said cheerfully.

"Fine . . . fine," my lawyer muttered and the line went dead.

Years ago, during one of my brief jail visits, an old man in the cell next to mine claimed that everything, even the most evil and senseless acts of violence, must have some redemptive meaning. Otherwise the universe would be absurd. The old man was in for killing his daughter's kitten and nailing its body to her bedroom door. I was in for public urination. He would bail out that night. I would have to wait until morning. We were drinking tequila and orange juice smuggled into the police station. I stared at him drunkenly as the police dispatch radio chattered in the background and all I could manage was, "Yeah, so what's your point?"

I'm not a cynic. Not really. I find the notion that the universe is absurd to be a great comfort. Absurdity is head and shoulders above malevolence. After Dickie and Dr. Trout called me I set the phone back on the wall and looked around for someone who could blow up the balloon.

Jane Marie was standing on a short stepladder taping a banner above the doorway. The banner was white freezer paper painted with horns and puppies. In bright blue letters it read "HAPPY 42 TODD!!!" Jane Marie was wearing her white painter coveralls, her glossy black hair pulled back in a red bandanna. Her nephew Bob was standing beneath her with his cheeks bulged out and his young face turning scarlet, trying to blow up another particularly tough balloon. As his face darkened from red to a frightening dark blue, the balloon became a tiny bulb in his one good hand. He immediately reached for it with the prosthetic hook on his other hand and the balloon broke.

"Goddamn it to hell!" the boy said.

"Hush," Jane Marie murmured as she taped the last corner of the banner to the wall.

"I hate this fucking hook," the boy said in a low voice that I'm not sure he intended anyone to hear.

"That's another quarter," Jane Marie said to him. "If you guys keep swearing like that I'll be able to retire to French Polynesia in no time."

"I agree with young Bob," I told Jane Marie. "That hook sucks. Why couldn't they put something useful on the end of his arm, like a compressed-air fitting? Then we could blow up these fucking balloons."

Young Bob started to titter nervously and gave me his mechanized "thumbs up" with the hinge of his prosthetic hand.

"Cecil." Jane Marie stepped down from the ladder and closer to me. "He's only seven years old. He's got to know that words mean something. You've had such a foul mouth for so long you don't hear the words anymore, but he's going to get in real trouble if he uses language like that at the wrong time."

Young Bob and I stared at each other, plotting. " 'Sucks' is not a bad word," I said finally. "I bet I could use it in a proper sentence at any given moment."

Jane Marie rolled her eyes, but then pushed against me, putting her arms around my waist. "Now you owe me *fifty* cents."

"All right," I said, and kissed her lightly on the lips. I listened for a moment to the gulls wheeling outside the window.

Jane Marie has been staying with me in my little house over the channel. Young Bob and his mother live across the street in an apartment over the coffee shop. For the last six months the five of us had been sharing meals together. The meals started as a social gathering but as the money became scarce we needed to pool our resources so we share our homes and food.

Jane Marie is the woman who is currently, if somewhat tentatively, in love with me. She does not think the universe is absurd. She is a scientist and a salesperson. She advises people what kinds of games to play and she offers a catalog to choose games from. For her, the universe is an endless possibility of bids and points. Malevolence comes from people who have to cheat or, sometimes, from a confusion of the rules. I like to look at her. Her face, her body: As beautiful and unexpected as finding one of Degas's ballerinas standing by the change machine at a laundromat. Since I know I don't deserve Jane Marie, it feels like cheating every time I touch her. Now I kissed her again and shuddered, wondering just how much I was going to have to suffer in the future for being so happy right at that moment.

"Where's the birthday boy?" I leaned away from her.

She scowled. "I don't really know. I called him at work and they said it was the middle of his shift but Todd wasn't there. The girl I talked to sounded funny, like she didn't really want to speak to me."

"They probably gave him his birthday off. He's walking his trap line with Wendall." Wendall was a pit bull–boxer mix Todd adopted a year or so ago. They had a circuit around town of places where they could stop and chat and find a cookie or some meat scraps.

I grabbed my coat off the hook by the stove. "I'll look for him on my way. I've got to run down to the Pioneers' Home and see my shrink."

"Your shrink. Why?"

"Oh, he's got somebody who wants to hire me to kill someone."

"You do that?" Young Bob was gaping up at me, confused and thrilled.

"No," I said in my most adult voice, making sure he knew I was serious. Then I turned back to Jane Marie. "But how can I pass up talking to him? How many times does your psychiatrist call you for a contract killing?"

"Just be careful," she called after me, as I turned to walk down the stairs to the street-level entrance of the house. "Don't start talking crazy stuff. It's very bad luck, Cecil. Especially if it's about murder."

Jane Marie has experience with crazy stuff and murder, so I take her worrying seriously and I don't tease her about it.

Outside, the spring air was warm and rich with the smells of commerce in this island town. The fish plants down the street were processing black cod, and the gulls and eagles were busy working the air above the outfall pipes in the channel. As I walked past the coffee shop, an eagle was gliding just over the ridge line of the native meeting house. The sun caught every feather of her wings and chest. I could see the musculature ripple under the feathers as she adjusted her wings for more altitude. I could see the yellow irises of her eyes as she turned her head toward the channel. A flurry of crows on the rim of a garbage can scattered. I smelled sour beer and coffee as I walked past my favorite bar and waved at the barmaid who was carrying a tray full of glasses back behind the bar. She waved back at me and when I stopped, she smiled sweetly, waving me on . . . to keep walking.

I thought of Angela Ramirez. I couldn't imagine I was going to get much of a case out of her death. I understood that she was dirt-poor and I doubted her family could interest any lawyer in a wrongful death case against William Flynn. Angela had been drinking heavily because her second husband Simon had left her. Simon Delaney was a dark-haired Irishman who worked the docks in Sitka and Dutch Harbor. He had hung with a large dark man named Marcus. Marcus and Simon had tried to unionize one of the fish plants without much success. Marcus moved back to Dutch Harbor. I don't know what happened to Simon. I just know Angela was left in that trailer with the two children of her first marriage.

I had seen Angela a few days before her murder, walking out of a bar trying to collect herself but unable to. She'd stumbled and fallen off the curb into the street. I'd helped her up. She accused someone of pushing her, then she invited me for a drink. I told her I couldn't. She laughed ruefully as if her invitation had been a joke, as if everything had been a joke. She pushed her black hair out of her eyes and returned into the bar. On the afternoon of the shooting, the neighbors heard her screaming as if she were beating her kids. They called 911 and told the cops Angela had left the trailer with a gun. The aid car took the kids, one boy and one girl, to the hospital, where they learned later that day their mother had been shot to death.

This case had possibilities but it would take work, because even for a small town this was not a very "sexy" killing. It didn't strike that resonant chord on the gossip circuit. Maybe it was just too heavy on the brutality and too light on the fairy tale. That is: too real. The perpetrator was not vile enough and the victim needed to be more charismatic to really make it into crime lore. Angela Ramirez was drunk, poor, and of Mexican heritage. She had abused her children, and she had a pistol in her hand when she was killed. William Flynn was an ancient, almost certainly indigent, white man with a pathetic motive for homicide and no deep pockets. These are bad facts for trying to wring money out of a case. For, as much of it as there is, regular old brutality just doesn't pay. That's why there are more private detectives on TV than there are in real life.

But the truth was I would do almost anything to whip these meager facts into some kind of case. Being a private investigator in a small town in Alaska is not the greatest career move. I don't advise it. Crime and mayhem come in spurts. My sister was a high-powered defense and plaintiff's attorney before she became a professor. When I worked for her we were in demand all over the state. We hardly ever did a case in the same town twice. I actually had a good reputation for criminal defense investigations, mostly because I have a florid imagination and could always think of some explanation for crime that would include innocence and indignation. But I had a degree in philosophy from Reed College. Well,

almost had a degree: I did attend college. I had meditated
in Asia, sung in southern gospel choirs, and once ran naked
around an entire city block of New York City without being
arrested. But I have never been a law enforcement officer or
a security guard and *those* are the kinds of credentials most
insurance companies and plaintiff defense firms are looking
for when they want an investigator. I used to get a call for every major homicide in the state, wherever it took place. But
there is a new young guy in Anchorage who has taken care
of that. He is fit and smart and looks great in a suit and tie.
He has a cellular phone and a bank of computers. He is ex-
military and has an MBA. He's a nineties kind of dick: efficient and billable. I haven't had a case in three months. I've
tapped out my sister for loans, and yesterday I saw a young
woman from the bank taking Polaroid pictures of my house.
The realtors have organized a phone tree in anticipation of
the foreclosure. My banker could refinance but she doesn't
like my prospects. I should get out with my equity, she says,
and make room for someone who could make good use of
industrial waterfront property.

But I wouldn't kill anybody for money. No matter
how much I needed it. I'm not the man for it. My memory
is too good. I wouldn't want to relive over and over the sight
of some poor fool going down under the weight of his own
blood. Then there would be all the stories about it afterward.
I have been in jail just long enough to know that killing someone almost always ends in a lifelong litany of justifications.
"I didn't mean it." "I was drunk." Or "The bastard was going
to get me first. What was I supposed to do?" For some pris-
oners, a killing, or at least the fact of the killing, becomes the
one immovable object in an otherwise fluid and corruptible
memory. The corpse is the reef they sit on day after day, talking about how inevitable their lives have become. Even when
someone comes by to pull them off the reef, these guys wave
them off.

My clients don't understand why I don't carry a gun and I try to explain to them. I don't carry a gun because I don't want to kill anyone. That's really it. It's not because I'm particularly virtuous or sensitive. No. It's because if I kill someone I'll go to prison for it. No one is going to believe my bullshit stories about why I had to do it. A corpse always has more credibility than I do.

An old friend of mine who I met in jail tries to talk me out of this all the time. He says that by not carrying a gun I'm giving over the field to the bad people who do. He says, "Cecil, you have the right. The good guys need to be better armed than the bad guys." This has a nice ring to it as long as you have it absolutely clear who the good guys are. That's where I've always been a little fuzzy.

I have defended enough killers to know that the only way to get away with murder is to either (A) wrap your client in immutable goodness; (B) wrap the corpse in tragic but undeniable badness; or (C) throw your hands up and tell the jury the police did such a terrible investigation that we are unable to make sense of the evidence against the backdrop of this goofy and corrupt world. If I kill someone I'm afraid none of these defenses are going to help me. No dead person could be that bad and the world, no matter how absurd, is just not *that* goofy and corrupt.

So I was empty-handed when I turned the corner near the bicycle shop and went up the ramp into the gardens of the Pioneers' Retirement Home. The tulips looked like Easter eggs on stems and the grass was a light green, having just been aerated so the roots could breathe the spring air. Alice Duke was standing by the statue of the prospector. I could tell she was wearing her nightgown under her wool overcoat. She was smoking a Lucky Strike and feeding bread crusts to the birds. Alice had been born in 1913 in Ohio. Her grandpa had fought in the Civil War. As she flipped out the last of her crusts I heard a weird electronic beeping and Alice pulled a cellular phone from her pocket and started bellowing into it. The pigeons flew away in a bluster of feathers, dung, and crumbs. I hurried through them.

Dr. Trout, my personal psychiatrist and salmon fishing advisor, was standing on the sun porch. "Hey, man, you're looking good," he said, as he patted me on the shoulder in an acceptable professional way.

"Thanks. That really means something, coming from you." Dr. Trout usually dressed like a homeless fisherman, mostly because he lived on his sailboat. He had been working in Alaska to save money for his around-the-world voyage. He was wearing a ragged wool halibut jacket and frayed jeans over rolled-down rubber boots. He was several thousand dollars away from being able to set sail. He was saving up to buy a rocket launcher so he could navigate through the pirates of the South China Sea. My psychiatrist is definitely a "Peace Through Strength" kind of guy.

"So how are things in Murder Incorporated?" I asked, as we walked in through the double doors and up to the ramps leading to the hospital care floor.

"Cecil, hush." He laughed and ducked his head to see if anyone could hear us. "You know how these people can be. We don't want to start any unnecessary gossip."

A woman in a motorized wheelchair came barreling around the corner and swerved toward the wall.

"On your left, God damn it!" the driver cackled as she sped down the hall out of sight.

"Right. I'll stick to the necessary gossip. How much will I get for killing the witness?" I asked him.

"Dickie wants you to see if you think there *is* another witness to the shooting." We stopped on the third-floor landing. Dr. Trout gestured vaguely down the hall to the left to indicate his patient was just down there and then lowered his voice.

"He was very close to the woman who was . . . killed."

The doctor was clearly uncomfortable with the word. "She used to visit him here with her kids. She used to bring him flowers and she visited regularly. The kids, too. On the afternoon of the shooting she had told William she was going to leave Sitka. It was very upsetting to William. Now the children are in the hospital and their mother is dead."

"How is he answering questions?" I asked the doctor.

"Like many people his age, William's long-term memory of things that happened long ago is very full and quite detailed. But as to what happened recently, that is very spotty. As a result he has confusion with continuity. Old memories erupt onto his most recent perceptions. We have our work cut out for us."

My doctor took a file folder from a nurse and tapped it with the tips of his fingers. He frowned at me, then turned to look toward a window past the third-floor TV lounge. In the window I could see another bald eagle banking over the roof of the old post office building down toward the channel. In the lounge, a woman in a wheelchair was breathing from bottled oxygen and watching Vanna White flip over the vowels.

My doctor spoke from somewhere back in his memory. "He's a fascinating man . . . Mr. Flynn." We both watched the eagle disappear behind the window frame. Then my shrink turned back to me.

"He insists on talking to you, Cecil. He has said he wants you to kill someone. But when you listen to him, try not to focus on that. Of course, we don't want you killing anyone . . ."

"If you say he is not competent, that means he cannot do anything to aid in his own defense. Why am I talking to him at all?" I spread my hands. A nurse walked by and I shuddered at the funereal sound of her rubber soles on the tiles. Dr. Trout took my arm and we started down the hall. He slapped the file folder against his leg. We stopped outside a closed door. "Just listen to him, Cecil. Something profound is troubling him—"

"Yeah, I bet. Like the fact that he may be the oldest murderer on record," I interrupted, but Dr. Trout pushed on speaking as if to himself.

"I can't put my finger on it, Cecil. I don't want to treat him as if he were a child. He may still be competent, he just may be confused. He *has* lived through all of the twentieth century. No wonder he's a little agitated."

My doctor smiled down at me with some concern. "He can pay you for your time if that's what you're worried about. I'll back you up as long as your bills are reasonable."

"Billing is my best work," I joked, but Dr. Trout was not listening as he stared into his file, murmuring to himself again.

"William Flynn. . . . Born in Clinton, Iowa. He and his brother came to Alaska in the early twenties, but I'm not sure of any of the exact dates. They lived together for the rest of their lives until Tommy, that's the brother, died in . . . let's see . . . I can't find it here right now but he left the home in the late eighties, I think." Dr. Trout wore an expression of wonder. "The two brothers lived together for seventy years. Most of that time in a cabin up the coast. Now it's a wilderness area but it was their home for all that time."

He stopped speaking and stared down the hall to the window again. I imagine he was trying to chart the great distances that William Flynn and his brother had covered in a century. I watched him lean against William's door, daydreaming. The doctor had a short gray crew cut and a spring sunburn from being out in his boat. I touched his sleeve and he woke from his dream, then started to push on the door. He turned back suddenly.

"Let's try to avoid talking about politics." His whisper was urgent, his head close to mine.

"Politics?" I asked.

"Politics. Philosophy. Give it a wide berth. Otherwise, we'll be here all day." He pushed against the door and we walked in.

"William? William?" Dr. Trout said in a loud voice to the man in the wheelchair with his back to us. "I told you I'd bring him." The doctor turned to me ceremoniously and said, "Cecil, I'd like you to meet William Flynn."

William Flynn looked almost as he had when I had met him. Somehow he was more pale and sunken in on himself. His eyes were wider and less focused, and his left hand shook as it rested on the arm of the wheelchair. He had a full white beard, yet didn't give the impression of either God, Santa Claus, or Karl Marx. William Flynn had spent a great many years working out in the weather. His hands were scarred and were still the color of rough-sawn oak. Unlike old men who balance their skulls on stems, he had broad shoulders and his neck jutted up from the muscles of his torso. His hair was thick but the skin around his temples was a parchment that showed the maze of blood vessels. His right hand engulfed mine in a leathery grip and I held on to it for longer than might have been called for. It wasn't until after my grip tightened on his that I felt the quaver of his body his left hand betrayed. I saw in his blue eyes the distant haze of ice, the toehold of confusion and uncertainty. William Flynn was a very old man in a durable body. His soul was a weary traveler. Looking at him I began to feel uncomfortable, as if I were walking over a canyon on a narrow railroad bridge hearing a train whistle far down the line.

The room was cramped, with just enough space for the three of us, a bed, a dresser and a chair. Dr. Trout sat on the chair. William did not drop my hand. I sat down on the corner of the bed, knee to knee with the old man in his wheelchair. He pulled me in so close that I could smell his hair oil.

"Is Angela coming today?" His eyes searched the room, then my face.

"No, Mr. Flynn. Angela won't be coming," I said and tried to release my hand from his grip.

"Do I know you?" His voice had the timbre of an antique pump organ.

"We have met before," I told him.

"The hell you say. I'm sure that's so, I just don't recall," William murmured, looking around, a little disoriented.

"There's no real reason you would remember. It was maybe twenty years ago. I was working on a fishing boat for the summer. It was a troller owned by Don Chumley. We anchored near your place to work on gear and you gave us some vegetables from your garden."

William leaned forward, his expression brightening. "Chumley, you say. By God, I do remember that boat. The *Dixie*. It used to belong to John Adolfson. Stout old slab."

"That's the one. You look pretty much the same now as you did back then. 'Course you were getting around better."

William looked down at his wheelchair. He grimaced. "You know, young fella, I've been an old man longer than most people get to be human beings." He waved his hand as if brushing away a memory. "But Chumley, you say? I do recall him. Chumley was a good sort. He could catch fish, if I recall."

"That's true, and he was a decent boss."

"He gave you a good share, did he?" William asked. He was referring to the crew share the skipper of the boat was to give me. He was sitting in full sunshine now and as he spoke he began to look healthier and even mischievous.

"Oh, it wasn't that much of a share, but I was green, you know. I suppose I wasn't worth that much."

"I bet he got another green crewman that next season?"

"Yeah. I think he did."

William wheeled over to the dresser and leaned over to pull out the bottom drawer. The drawer bumped against the foot supports on his chair. He carefully folded back a wool blanket and uncovered a square tin box. He brought it out onto his lap.

"Did I tell you how the Japanese fish?" he asked suddenly. "About how those Japanese fishermen would tie a cord around the necks of birds: Cormorants . . . we got them out here. Did I tell you about that? They tie the cord tight so the birds can't swallow the fish. They send 'em off on a job and as soon as those birds catch a fish, the fishermen jerk them back up."

The doctor caught my eye. He was making a cutting gesture with his hand across his throat. He pointed to his wristwatch. William saw him too but pretended not to see.

"I think you did tell me that one—" I offered but William rushed on.

"The birds can't swallow. Fisherman jerks 'em up by the cord and keeps the damn fish." He waved his hands around dismissively. "Oh, maybe the fisherman gives him some guts, or a little piece of the tail or something, but the damn bird only gets the scraps."

I nodded and when I looked at the doctor again he had his head buried in his hands. William leaned forward now with a wild look in those blue eyes.

"Well, sir, those cormorants learned to speak Japanese. They got plumb indignant about the share of the profits they were getting. Damned if they didn't organize the Protective Association of Cormorants. Well, the Japanese Fisherman's Association didn't like the idea of higher wages, but finally agreed to give them birds little pieces of paper. Then the cormorant could buy as much fish as they had paper for. You know, this sounded pretty good to those birds: Fish guts cost so many pieces, tails so much, and it was all open to however much each bird earned. This sounded like freedom.

But the fishermen kept raising the price of guts, so the birds went on strike. Oh, the birds went pretty hungry, but finally they got ten percent more paper than when they started. But by the end of the strike the fishermen had raised the price of fish ten percent, saying, 'Supply and demand, boys! Your strike made the fish harder to get so the cost went up. It's only natural.' "

By this time the doctor was clearing his throat and beginning to get to his feet, but William went on.

"But one old cormorant stood up and said that this whole cord-around-the-throat system . . . the ring and all . . . had to go. This old bird said the cormorants didn't need the damn fishermen. He said if all cormorants felt the same they could be their own bosses. Well, the birds that had worked out this deal with the pieces of paper and all the increases and everything were pretty pissed off. They said, 'We can't just junk the social system that we live by. What will we do without the system?' So they turned their backs on the crazy cormorant and got busy for another round of increases in the slips of paper."

William cocked his head and looked at me. "This sawbones . . . he thinks I'm a crazy old bird."

The doctor knew enough not to speak. He just looked down at his file, then straight into William's eyes and waited.

"Tommy and I were truly free, you see. It just seems crazy. We owned our own boat. We *owned* our own means of production. A boat and a garden. We were strange all right but not crazy."

William pried open the lid of the tin box and re-trieved a yellowed envelope. From it he fanned out an assort-ment of bills: twenties and fifties. These bills were very old and their age gave them more substance. They seemed solid, like gold . . . or my house.

"Simon Delaney," William Flynn said and then sat

silent. The trees beyond his window moved with the wind. A truck with a bad exhaust went down the street. I kept looking at the money.

"Simon Delaney was Angela's husband. He knows about it. Find Simon and I'll give you a better share than Chumley ever did. I'll give you all the worthless slips of paper you want."

He studied me, his ancient eyes narrowing, weighing something in his mind. "Can you find Simon Delaney?" he asked me unexpectedly.

I hesitated. "I suppose I could."

His eyes locked on mine. "You look stout. Are you honest?"

"Yes, sir, I am," I said without hesitation. I wasn't going to hedge, just in case he turned out to be more like God after all.

"Do you drink beer or whiskey?" He seemed to be ticking off a list in his head.

"Well, sir, I have. Pretty heavy. But not today and I don't think I will tomorrow."

He leaned back into his chair. "The booze will dehorn a man. Take his mind off his business."

The doctor was writing something in the file. I looked to him for help and he smiled up at me in that irritating, "What do *you* think?" look they must teach in psychiatry school.

William spoke slowly this time and for the first time didn't look at me directly. His voice had a low quaver. "Have you accepted Jesus Christ as your personal savior?"

I stared at him and grimaced, wondering just where this test of my credentials was going, but I knew it would do no good to dance around this question. "No," I told him. And then remembering one of the only old labor songs I had ever known, I added, "I'll have my pie here, if that's all right."

William looked over at the doctor and smiled. He raised his left hand.

"That's right!" The hand waved uncontrollably in a wild gesture. "I won't have no Bible-thumping drunks. Oh, the bastards say this and that, but all they want is to separate you from what's yours. I won't have it."

A cloud rolled past the sun and the shadow breathed into the room. William sagged down into his chair and instantly he seemed more frail. The doctor cleared his throat, but William waved him off.

William slowly rolled his chair a few inches back against the open window. The window looked out to the back garden of the home. I could see one of the maintenance men picking up an empty pint of wine someone had thrown under the rhododendron. On the bedside stand was a black-and-white photo in a silver frame. The photo was of two young men standing arm in arm on the back deck of an old-style trolling boat.

"This girl Angela and her children visited me. They brought me flowers," William said.

"Did they?" I wasn't really asking.

"She was going to leave me alone. Take them all away. It was that town killed her."

"Killed who?" I said.

"It started a long time ago. Everybody has forgotten about it. The boys said it would be all right. I didn't want to have anything to do with it but I went up on the hill anyway. They said it was self-defense. I don't know. I really don't know." His voice trailed off. All I could hear was the scratching of the doctor's pencil.

William took a breath. "Flowers and beautiful girls always remind me of one another. You know what I mean? The girl kept coming. Kept bringing me the flowers. The flowers are a kind of company, you know. She was always friendly. She never asked for a thing. I tried to give her things she needed, but she wouldn't have any of it. She was going away."

Here he stared down at his hands in his lap. His lips started to quiver but no tears came. He gestured around the room with his shaking hand.

I said, "The police say you had the gun used to kill her. Is that so?"

"Goddamn gun! We should never have had that god-damn gun, it just brought everybody grief." His chest was heaving. "Up on that hill in the summertime there were always flowers," he said. He was whispering almost under his breath: "Wild rose, honeysuckle, ocean spray, ox-eyed daisies . . ."

I looked around his room and saw that every flat surface had a container of flowers. There was a rusty red Hills Brothers coffee can with a sprig of a wild crabapple branch, and above his sink were two dark blue medicine bottles that could have been dug out of a dump. One held a daffodil and the other flowering currant. In the sink it looked as if a child had dumped an apron of dandelions.

But it was all wrong, for even though the flowers moved through the changing light that the rest of us were in, they were all dead: burnt paper and melted straws. The sinkful of dandelions looked like a handful of dead bees swept from a windowsill.

"They just stopped coming. Those children," William Flynn said. "That gun killed their mother just as she was going to leave me. Their mother, you know?"

"Did you kill Angela Ramirez?" I asked as routinely as possible. After all, neither the doctor nor I was going to testify against the old man.

William Flynn would not look at me. He knew what I had asked. He knew the difference between right and wrong. And he was able to speak. I was feeling more optimistic about a decent defense trial: long and billable. Then he said softly,

"She loved those children." The sun broke through again and we could hear the clinking of glass in the plastic bag as the maintenance man outside threw garbage in the Dumpster. "She didn't have any money. Who is going to take care of those kids now? Simon Delaney? The cops?"

William's head was shaking back and forth. He was talking to someone, someone far back in his memory. "We were all children, I suppose, but when they killed those boys it tore the town apart."

"What boys, Mr. Flynn?" I looked at the doctor but he didn't speak.

"Warren Grimm" was all William said. Then, "Do you know him?"

"No, I don't," I answered politely, and behind William's shoulder I saw the doctor shrug, meaning he didn't know either.

I could hear the TV distantly down the hall and a Swainson's thrush sang in the ash tree in the garden. Finally William pushed back in his chair and wiped his nose on his sleeve.

"Angela was from Mexico. Or her family was. She met that boy down in Washington. That boy's a nephew, of some sort. He's a regular mutt. His grandma was Chinese, worked at the pool hall. Simon Delaney. That's the boy, did I tell you that?"

I nodded yes and William kept on.

"Angela's family was picking peas and planting trees around that goddamn town."

"Seattle?" I offered.

"Centralia. It's the goddamnedest town." His voice was fierce. He looked wildly around the room as if visited by a nightmare. "It rains there and the rivers flood. Then all spring it smells like dead bodies."

His eyes focused out into some middle distance that was very far from me.

"All the boys wanted was clean blankets. By God, that's all. All her people wanted was toilets they could use. Those others should have stayed home. It always starts as talk, talk, talk and then there are dead people and goddamn lawyers. I won't have any more of it." He banged his fist on top of the tin box and the chair shook on the floor. His eyes were shut.

"Mr. Flynn, why do you want me to find Simon Delaney?"

William Flynn lurched forward over the tin box that was still on his lap and grabbed my hands so tightly they ached.

"He knows everything. He knows about the boys and about Tommy. They said it was self-defense but . . . but nobody believed them."

There was a long pause. I heard a nurse's cart roll by his door. I heard a siren across the roof of the bookstore on the other side of the street. William still gripped my hands in his.

"How can I find Simon Delaney?" I asked him.

"Have you ever heard of Ole Hanson?" His expression as he looked at me was unimaginably sad, a lifetime of hurt. He took long damp breaths and let my hands go.

"No, I haven't," I said, my own voice starting to quaver.

"I don't know where he is now. I don't know. He could have saved those boys, but he didn't. He didn't . . ."

The shadow was back in the room. The garbage truck was grinding and clattering in the street and the thrush was gone along with the siren. William's chest heaved up and down.

"They searched that river and they never found him, or me either. We could have helped those boys. I'm sure we could have, but we never did."

"Who didn't they find, Mr. Flynn?" I asked.

There was another long pause. I was about to either give up or repeat the question. Then William spoke.

"That boy knows. He knows everything. Simon knows about Angela. Simon was born in that town. He drank that water. He listened to all that talk and it ended up with the guns and that girl getting shot down."

William tried to stifle his sobs, but they heaved up from his lungs.

"All these flowers are dead. I know that. I'm not crazy." His left hand flapped crazily around his head in a gesture to draw the entire room into the circle of his grief.

I waited a full minute in silence. The doctor made more notes and William studied the picture of the two young men by his bed. Then I leaned forward and touched his right hand. "What do you want, Mr. Flynn?"

"If you find Ole Hanson, then you'll find Simon Delaney. Maybe Simon Delaney would take you to Ole Hanson, I don't know. I just don't care. Find 'em both."

"Why?"

"Because I want us all to be buried together." On the bundles of old bills, his hands trembled.

I sat up straight and the bed springs creaked. "But Simon Delaney is a young man, Mr. Flynn. I doubt he's much more than thirty."

"We all have to be in the ground together."

"Why?"

"I want to be buried next to him," William Flynn hissed through clenched teeth.

Dr. Trout finally spoke up. "Where do you want to be buried, William?"

William craned his neck around to look at the doctor. "I want to be buried above the tide line, far away from that town. We're all killers, but good people can still hang a dead man."

Outside, the garbage truck roared up the street, leaving the voice of the thrush to bob up in the silence. William Flynn looked me dead in the eye. "They can kill a man twice. Don't you think they can't, Mr. Younger. I saw it happen."

Chapter Two

The doctor slapped the file against his leg, looking forward as we walked down the hall. He said absently, "The old man is confused, Cecil. I'm sorry I brought you here. He's clearly not competent." Then he spoke urgently to me as if I were helping him form these words. "But it's interesting, don't you think? Back there he was able to draw on two frames of memory in one conversation."

"Are these memories? Or is he just making this stuff up?"

"Well, to some extent all memory is just made up. Memories are the sensory impressions stored in our brains. We have pictures, smells, music, words, bruises, kisses," he waved his hand vaguely around his head, "all stored in our brain circuits. Every piece affects every other one in storage. When we draw a memory out of storage we search for the right language that makes sense, not only for the audience but for all of this interior information that makes up our current self. William Flynn's storage system is very old. The stored bits of information have to fit the format, the emotional needs, of the person who is now recalling them."

A nurse walked by and disappeared into the stairwell. "Just think of all he's witnessed," the doctor went on. "Hell, there were Gettysburg and Antietam veterans telling stories in their wheelchairs when he was a young man." Dr. Trout shook his head absently. Then he snapped his attention back to me. "This is all very shorthand, but what you were probably asking was: Can we believe him? The answer is yes, at least on some level. William is not being intentionally deceptive. He is accurately representing his desires and wishes. But he is clearly not competent to stand trial for murder."

The doctor turned away from me and stared out the window. The features on his face were troubled but set. "He can't stand a trial. A jury would never make any sense of him. He's like a time capsule: a nineteenth-century man left here . . . alone . . . ."

"Does he really want me to kill Simon Delaney?"

"I don't know." We watched the three ravens sitting on the power line running behind the Russian cathedral. A light wind ruffled the small feathers on their chests. "Really, what I think he wants you to do is to save somebody's life."

"Whose?"

"Angela Ramirez's maybe . . . probably. But also something happened in a river and some boys died. I think he wants you to save those boys' lives, too."

We watched as the raven on the left raised his hackles and barked furiously as a fourth one came to the wire. Dr. Trout continued, "William has made a connection between these two events: some tragedy in a river and the death of Angela Ramirez. There is some commonality there, so the unresolved force of the old one lends itself to the other. Of course he can't say that, so he finds a link, picks a person to blame, in this case, Simon Delaney. I think William wants Delaney dead to lay to rest not only Angela but those boys in the river. Obviously you're not going to kill Mr. Delaney." And my doctor looked at me for a long moment.

"Obviously," I said, snapping myself out of a fantasy. My doctor scowled at my tone of voice. "Anyway . . . I don't think Mr. Delaney is going to help William Flynn." A gust came and the wire swung; all four ravens took to the air and we were staring at the blank signature line of wire.

"Do you think Simon Delaney saw William kill Angela Ramirez?" I pushed ahead into the actual world.

The doctor shook his head. "I talked about this with Dickie. He hasn't passed all the police reports on to me yet, but apparently Delaney wasn't even on the island at the time of the shooting. Angela was killed on the twelfth and Delaney left on the ferry the night of the tenth." Pigeons wheeled around the old woman at the base of the statue in the front garden. My doctor sighed. "Well, again I'm sorry to get you involved. There is obviously nothing you can do." He turned and walked into the stairwell.

"I can find Delaney," I said as I thought about the realtors and about some yuppie building an art gallery in my house.

We stopped on the stairwell. The doctor looked both up and down and made sure no one was coming. His voice was low so as not to echo. "You could do that" was all he said, with the irritating tone that psychiatrists keep in their reservoir of dirty tricks.

I followed the doctor back out onto the covered porch of the home. He stopped again and we watched the white bluffs of clouds out above the westward islands.

"He doesn't have any living relatives. He's got no plans. He wants to be at rest. That's certain." He turned to me and I was surprised that my doctor's eyes were urgent and sharply focused on mine. "I can keep him out of prison, long enough to find a place to bury him. But I frankly don't know what you can do to help."

"Do you think he killed Angela Ramirez?" I asked him.

The sun broke out momentarily and light off the water dappled around him. The doctor took in a long breath. "If we're lucky, we live a long time, Cecil. We get to watch everyone we ever loved die. We get to have the life slowly pinched out of our body and we get a whole lifetime to imagine our own death. William Flynn desperately needed the company that Angela and her children provided. I think when she told him she was leaving Sitka to follow her husband, William became . . . extremely agitated." He stopped speaking and turned back to me.

"Let's just assume he killed her. The police say he had the gun. Some people claim he had been out of his room. He apparently told a nurse that Angela wasn't going to come back anymore after her last visit. But what's the point of putting a ninety-seven-year-old man in jail, Cecil? He's not going to live long enough to pay for what he did."

A stoop-shouldered man shuffled up the path into the gardens. A raven flew over and my eye caught on a bit of red thread trailing from the black bird's leg. I could hear the wind rush by the primary feathers on the wing. I focused on the bird until it disappeared.

"How did William know where to find her?" I asked the doctor. "How did he manage to pull it all off?"

"Ask Simon Delaney. He apparently knows." The doctor plodded on, not trying to hide his irritation.

This case was slipping away from me. I started a checklist in my mind.

"Where is Tommy Flynn buried? Why not just plant the old man next to his brother when the time comes?"

The doctor looked down at the file. "It's hard to say, Cecil. Nothing in William's file mentions him. He may not have even gotten along with him, after seventy-some years together. I don't know . . ." He held his index finger on a line near the bottom of the file. He looked up at me and his urgency was mixed with confusion. "There is a weird note here. In the margin it just says, 'known heirs: disputed.' I don't know what that is about. Tommy Flynn died here in the home. I thought." He was squinting at the file. "I can't find anything here about where he is buried."

The stoop-shouldered man came closer and I could see clearly now that it was my roommate. Todd was walking with his jacket pulled tight around his waist. He looked like a refugee from the Russian front. He saw me and flinched, then sat quickly on a bench. He sat so still I could tell he was trying to use his secret powers of invisibility.

"Well, let me talk to Dickie," I said and stretched as if waking up from a dream. "The old man wants me to find Delaney. But apparently it won't do him any good as far as his chances for a defense or a shot at a competency motion. Is that it?"

Dr. Trout nodded sadly. "That's it, Cecil. I'm sorry."

"Yeah, don't worry about it," I said, and stepped off the porch feeling dejected. The doctor waved the file and went back inside.

Toddy sat on the bench with the slumped shoulders and bulky form of a cartoon bear. He looked at the ground even though I know he was aware of my steps coming toward him.

"Hey, happy birthday, man. What are you doing here? I think they've got supper ready back at the house."

"I can't go home, Cecil." A fat pigeon pecked the toe of his foot and Todd watched it without moving.

"Why not?" I asked him.

"It's not . . . opportune."

"Opportune?"

He looked at me, his brown eyes swimming behind the thick lenses of his glasses. He had been crying. "Is that the right word, 'opportune'?"

"Just tell me what happened." I sat down next to him

and put my arm around his shoulders and Todd sagged, letting his breath out, knowing, I suppose, that the time he was not looking forward to had come.

"I got fired," he said flatly. The pigeon fluttered up beside him and stood on the back of the bench next to his shoulder. Toddy turned toward the bird and held his index finger out.

"Fired?" I said. "How can that be? You were doing great at the burger place. Your social worker had set everything up. I didn't think you were having any trouble."

Toddy grimaced and shook his head. Tears winked out of the sides of his eyes and he was groaning as if he had been hit in the gut. I felt stupid because I could tell he was taking my stupid disbelief as criticism. I patted him and pulled him closer.

"What did the manager say?" I asked him softly.

"He just said I talked too much to the customers and wasn't following directions carefully enough."

I stared down at my own feet and Toddy kept poking his finger toward the fat bird by his shoulder.

"Well, he's an asshole," I said.

Toddy looked at me, almost purely aghast. "Oh, no, Cecil. Mr. Wooster's a very nice man. He is very efficient and productive. He's gone to hamburger school and everything. He knows all of the procedures by heart. He doesn't have to look them up or anything."

Toddy stared at me as if wondering how I could say anything bad about the man who had fired him. The pigeon flew away. Todd took a deep breath and went on. "Mr. Wooster said I talked too much to the customers. He said that it was taking too much time and that I wasn't there to be friendly but I was supposed to be efficient."

An old man in a blue windbreaker came shuffling slowly down the steps on his way to the bar. He lightly tapped the back of the bench as he made his way past us.

"Well, forget it tonight," I told Toddy. "It's your birthday. We can have a great dinner and then tomorrow we'll get it figured out." I slapped his knee and stood up.

"I can't go home," he said.

"Why in the heck not?"

"I don't have my clothes," he said almost inaudibly. Toddy briefly opened his coat and I could see that he didn't have a shirt on.

"The pants are mine, of course," he said earnestly, wanting to reassure me. "I paid for them when I began my employment. But the shirt, the hat, and the tie and tie tack are all company property. When Mr. Wooster said I had to leave, he said I couldn't get my last check until I brought the clothes back fully cleaned. Well, Cecil, I went across the street and took them to the cleaners. I gave them the clothes and I forgot that I didn't have any money and I wouldn't have any until I got that check. So I . . . so I . . ." His face contorted in a deep unhappiness. He started rocking back and forth, his mind easing away from this ragged and complicated life.

"Why didn't you just tell the people at the cleaners the situation? I bet they would have let you take the clothes across the street."

"I couldn't . . . I didn't."

I understood. We sat for a few minutes. The fuel barge moved slowly through the channel. I wasn't going to say any more about why he wouldn't ask because I knew I might have done—or not done—the same thing.

"Do you want me to go over and get your clothes?" I asked.

Todd didn't say a word. The fuel barge eased out of sight. The old man rounded the corner toward the bar and the fat pigeon circled the statue of the prospector and landed again at our feet.

"People think I'm stupid and ineffective, Cecil. They think I can't work." He took a deep breath as if he were going to say much, much more but instead he stopped and looked down the walk.

Jane Marie came walking quickly from the direction of our house. She had a bundle under her arm and she waved gaily as she saw us sitting on the bench. Toddy's eyes brightened.

Jane Marie looked like a movie star in real life. That is, she wasn't perfect and youthful, her skin showed the weather and her face was creased, but her eyes and her body were sparked by an energy that attracted attention.

She walked up to us, set the bundle in Toddy's lap, and squatted by his knees, her hands reaching out to his on his lap. "Hey, you guys, we've got quite a party warming up at home." Her voice was gay. She squeezed Todd's hands but he looked down, grimacing again as if he couldn't stand to explain himself anymore.

"Eva at the cleaners called me. She was worried that you didn't come get your uniform. I called your job and they told me what happened."

Todd wouldn't look at her. He was twisting away from her but she wouldn't let go of his hands.

"I brought you your nicest shirt," Jane Marie said. "I think it makes you look handsome, like Bruce Willis. Don't you think so, Cecil?"

"Absolutely. Bruce Willis." I nodded. "A smarter, more capable Bruce Willis," I added. Todd started fighting against a smile. He looked at Jane Marie and at the shirt.

"Thank you. I greatly appreciate your bringing me the shirt."

"You're welcome." She nodded, then reached up and stroked his cheek. "Don't worry about the job tonight, Todd. Not tonight, okay?" Todd looked at her blankly, as if surprised and stunned by her love. I knew exactly how he felt.

Jane Marie went on. "I mean, a job is one thing. We'll

all have dozens of jobs in this life. But a party—" she gestured to the sky with her palms, "a party like this! Why, there will be nothing like it."

The three of us stood up. I motioned Todd to the porch of the Pioneers' Home. The covered area offered an out-of-the-way place for him to put on his shirt.

Jane Marie stood next to me and we watched him lumber up the steps. She slipped her hand in mine.

"Can you get him his job back, Cecil?" She squeezed my hand.

"Me?" I looked at her. "I don't pull a lot of weight in the burger industry."

"But they have this program. They say all the time how they provide employment for people . . . what do they call it? Entry-level workers and challenged citizens."

"They're just low-paying jobs with a lot of turnover," I offered lamely.

"I know you can do something." She moved in closer to me, looking trusting and earnest. She rubbed the back of my hand with her thumb. Her breath was sweet with tomato sauce and red wine. It's people like Jane Marie who make being a cynic hard work.

"I'll see what I can do. I'll just run over, get his uniform, and take it back. I'll talk to the guy."

Toddy was coming down the stairs, his head still down and with that same flat-footed gait of a kid who expects a whipping. Jane Marie moved over to him and put her arm around him. She kissed his cheek and then danced with him down the sidewalk. She called out to me, "Don't be too long, Cecil. The wild rumpus is about to begin: spaghetti, lemonade, mashed potatoes, and corn on the cob."

Todd jerked his head up, looking at her in wonder. "It's your birthday, fella! We've blown out all the stops," Jane Marie told him.

The ravens hopped the tree line while I walked up

over the hill through the graveyard on my way to Todd's former place of employment. I took a detour down off the hill to where Angela Ramirez's trailer was still parked. The mountain ash tree was leafing out. The blocks under the galvanized trailer tongue were sinking into the muck. There was a fire in a barrel out in front. The trailer door was open. A man stood stooped in the doorway. He was barrel-chested and dark-skinned. He had frayed black pants and suspenders over his clean hickory shirt. He blew his nose into a red bandanna. His eyes were red. When he saw me, he instantly stiffened. He had tiny eyes that narrowed like a bear scanning the brush. I paused unthinkingly and stumbled slightly on a bicycle near the trash barrel. In a moment that passed suddenly, the man's body sagged and his face curled into a grimace. Then he turned away, disappearing into the trailer. I could hear the frame squeaking against the leaf springs.

By the time I made it back to my house, the birthday party was well under way. It was just getting dark and the light from my open door spilled out onto the narrow waterfront street. I had passed six Filipino workers from the cold storage plant three doors down. A couple of them were still in their rain gear and were eating spaghetti from paper bowls. The others sat on the tailgate of a truck sharing a cigarette and stretching their arms over their heads. As I passed, one called out.

"Hey, Cecil, tell Toddy happy birthday, man. I might be over later after I get off shift."

"Okay, Nino," I said. But truthfully I wasn't in a very festive mood. I hadn't done much good at the burger place. Even though I got the uniform from the cleaners they wouldn't accept it back at the restaurant. Apparently Todd himself had to sign it in, and only he could pick up his last check. All of this was told to me by the assistant manager, who appeared to be about fifteen years old. He had shaved sometime in the last few days and several of his pimples were glazed over with scabs. He used the word "protocol" and I almost started weeping.

For some reason I started thinking about the movie *Five Easy Pieces,* when Jack Nicholson scattered the glasses off the table. In the movie, the snotty waitress wouldn't bring him wheat toast so to show the audience that people of artistic temperament no longer had to put up with authoritarian capriciousness, Jack threw glasses and broke crockery. As the assistant manager of the burger place started telling me about how generous he had been with Todd, and how his company had made an extra effort in hiring challenged citizens, that scene flashed through my mind and I remembered how I had always felt sorry for that grouchy waitress. I mean, here's Jack Nicholson's character. He's having sex with Susan Anspach AND Sally Struthers, and still he has to make a tired woman clean up broken glass because she didn't get his order right. That movie is probably the only reason I didn't punch the assistant manager.

I actually apologized to the assistant manager for the inconvenience, and as I carried the plastic-wrapped uniform shirt over my shoulder I knew I was kidding myself. I would never have punched that kid in a million years, and I realized that scene in the movie had been made for people like me: passive-aggressive wimps who only fantasize about being artists and sending our wheat toast back.

The mudroom off the street was piled with coats and rain gear: rubber boots, boat slippers and expensive leather sandals were shucked on the floor. I hung Todd's uniform shirt up on a peg next to the hot water heater, then walked upstairs to where the party was in full swing: the hum of people talking and laughing, the Mills Brothers singing "Glow, Little Glowworm" in the background. The lights were draped with Chinese lanterns and the room was cut by a haze of fruity colors and odd angles of shadow. The room was shoulder to shoulder with the people who wanted to wish Toddy well. Bob the Fisherman, who had promised he wouldn't get drunk, was talking to the young woman who was Todd's caseworker. Bob the Fisherman was apparently drinking coffee from his insulated traveler cup. Bob started scratching his neck when he saw me, and by the way he was pulling his ratty-looking beret down over his eyes I figured he had been slipping something into his coffee. Not that I cared. Bob was a fun drunk, at least until two in the morning. He would be out of my house before the furniture needed breaking. I was just hoping he wasn't going to say anything wacky to the caseworker, who had always been shaky on Toddy staying at my house. In the corner, Todd was sitting on the couch opening presents. Young Bob was hovering over Todd, reaching in to pull bits of tape from the packages with his prosthetic hook. A kid from the neighborhood named Otis brushed Young Bob's hand away. Todd was painstakingly slow in unwrapping his gifts, mostly for the pleasure of watching the two children squirm and wiggle for the gifts. Finally he gave the package over to Otis and another to Young Bob, saying he wasn't able to get the knots himself. As I turned into the kitchen alcove I heard the flurry of tearing paper as "Love Shack" by the B-52's came on.

Jane Marie was cutting lemons, and her sister Priscilla was stirring a large pot of spaghetti. When I came in close, Jane Marie bumped her hip against mine.

"Hey, sailor, want to squeeze some lemons?"

"I'd like to get drunk," I said, not looking her in the eyes.

"Cool!" she said. "Can I watch you vomit out your nose and try to commit suicide in the morning?"

"Gross." Priscilla grimaced.

"Come on, Cecil," Jane Marie swung a glass around and put it to my lips, "have some lemonade. After cake, we'll have some mashed potatoes, get rid of these clowns, and have wild sex until daylight."

"Does that mean I can't get drunk?" I took a sip of the lemonade.

"Hey, I'll never fuck another drunk. I have my standards." Jane Marie kissed me hard on the lips. Her lips tasted sugary with blue icing. We bumped teeth in the middle of the kiss because we both started to smile.

Priscilla shook her head slowly over the mouth of the pot. "Standards? What kind of standards allow you to sleep with this guy?"

Jane Marie looked at her sister and drank lemonade as if it were a glass of tequila in a Juárez whorehouse. Her eyes were smoky. "Priscilla, I'm telling you, this guy is great in bed and has no fear of death."

Priscilla shuddered. "Stop it. Please. There are some things I just can't think about."

Jane Marie laughed and spun me around. She rubbed my chin. "I know you weren't able to get Toddy's check. Don't worry about it tonight. We'll work it out, okay? You okay, Cecil?"

"Yeah, I'm okay."

"You want me to sit with you awhile?"

"Naw."

Just as I was moving in for another kiss, Pirate Ron grabbed my arm and jerked me around.

"Younger!" he growled. "Have you become a traitor to your sacred duty as a male?" Before I could answer, Ron tugged me out on the tiny balcony to watch over the barbecue grill where he was cooking a slab of freezer-burned halibut he had soaked in soy sauce. Pirate Ron worked in the fish plant but he was also the master of one of the ugliest steel-hulled fishing boats in the fleet. Tied up at the dock, his vessel looked like a ghost ship abandoned in the fog. It flew a skull-and-crossbones flag, and that was how Ron came by his name.

Someone played Spike Jones and then James Taylor

for some inexplicable reason. The night was calm, and the lights from the bridge sparkled in long smeary streaks on the water. A tugboat eased down the channel as I stood by the barbecue grill and listened to the gulls behind the rattle of the tug's engine. Pirate Ron ranted about "unexpected surges of weirdness that pulse through the culture of imperialistic Europeans" and how we were on the eve of "the big one. One of the weirdest in recorded time."

I wasn't listening, but that was okay because Pirate Ron doesn't expect anyone to listen to him anymore.

I knew Jane Marie had asked Ron to baby-sit me. It's hard for me not to drink at parties. As long as I stay engaged in a conversation or locked on a task I'm okay, but if I start to drift I eventually end up with a beer in my hand. Apparently Jane Marie was serious about wanting to have sex with me.

Eventually Pirate Ron was going to start talking about William Burroughs and I wanted to jump ship before that tape loop started to run. I held up my index finger and poked the fish, then told Ron I'd go and get a plate for the halibut. When I went back inside the big man from Angela Ramirez's trailer was standing as big as a statue of Simón Bolívar in my living room.

He was a tall man who looked used to stooping through doorways. He was standing awkwardly now, as Bob the Fisherman handed him a flimsy paper plate with strange blue birthday cake on it. As I walked into the room, the big man looked down at me beseechingly and said softly, "I'm looking for Mr. Younger. The detective . . . Cecil Younger?"

I looked around the house that was jammed with guests, half of whom I didn't recognize. I considered the bathroom as a place to talk to him, but then shuddered to think what might be going on in the bathroom.

We went downstairs, picked our way across the floor cluttered with red rubber boots, and I showed him to a room that I used for storing gear. It was a tiny shed built under the house. The shed sat on beams attached to the pilings with one end of the shed opening with double doors to the ramp where I pulled my skiff in and out of the water. I moved my chain saw out of the way, nudged a broken oar into the corner with my foot, then sat down on a sawhorse. The big man looked around and finally sat on a round of firewood I had been using as a splitting block.

"I'm Cecil Younger," I said, and held out my hand.

"David Ramirez." He engulfed my hand. I looked at his tired face and could see that his eyes were still rimmed in red.

"I saw you walk by the trailer," David Ramirez said. "I was going to come see you. I didn't know who you were or I would have talked to you then."

"That's all right." I waved my hand as if shooing away an inconsequential gnat. "What do you need, Mr. Ramirez?"

Above us I could hear the thumping of feet on the floor and the muffled squelch of dance music. David Ramirez's body sagged in the way only a strong man's can, as if he were deflating, losing his vitality before my eyes. "My daughter, Angela . . . my daughter . . . she was the one killed . . ."

"Yes," I said, and then waited for whatever it was that was coming.

"I came up from Washington, from Centralia, to retrieve her things. To take the little children back to their grandmother . . . ."

The big man was struggling. As if the words secreted poison. The image of his daughter's death was growing toxic in his mind.

He pushed on. "I don't have any real argument with the police. I talked to the young man who . . . the young man who found her."

Inexplicably, an old chain for my saw fell off the vise

where it had been resting. It clattered on top of a fuel can and we both jerked, startled by the noise. Mr. Ramirez laughed at the absurdity of it all. Then he started to cry.

"Angela was drinking. But she wouldn't hurt those children. Every particle of those children . . . they were sacred to her. She wouldn't hurt them. I know that."

I shook my head and waited. Mr. Ramirez sat up straight, letting his big hands clench in his lap. I could sense his sadness sucking away into some imagined past or future. After a while, he stopped crying.

"I am concerned with Simon Delaney," he blurted out through clenched teeth. "I want to know where he is."

"I don't know." I shook my head. The dancing stopped on the floor above us. "Why do you want to find him?"

The big man's body trembled. He stood up abruptly, looking wildly around the shed as if he were waking up from a nightmare. He started for the door, stopped and picked up the chain saw chain, and put it lightly down on the vise. Then he turned back to me. "I have done all kinds of work, Mr. Younger. I have picked fruit and dug trenches. I've cut down trees. Now I help others to get work. I put crews together, you understand?"

I stared up at him and nodded. The music came back on upstairs. The floorboards of the shed squealed as Mr. Ramirez shifted his weight on the balls of his feet. He looked down at me as if he were scolding a puppy. "Simon Delaney does not work. Simon Delaney does not create anything for his family." David Ramirez struck out at the air with his arm. He bumped against my workbench. "Simon Delaney agitates and creates unhappiness. He caused this . . . . He caused what happened to my Angela."

"Do you blame him for Angela's death?"

"Yes . . ." He stared down at me and his tiny eyes were as impassive as a rag doll's . . . or a shark's.

"Are you going to hurt him if you find him?" I smiled up at him, begging, I suppose, for some light.

"I don't know what you're talking about," he muttered.

"Good," I said. "Because if I did find Simon Delaney for you and it resulted in a felony being committed, then we could both be charged with conspiracy. It's not something the DAs charge all by itself, but it would be added onto a list of charges so they could bargain it down to what they really want."

"I just want you to tell me where he is." David Ramirez's voice did not falter. His eyes did not flicker with any doubt or uneasiness. "I don't want you to talk to him. I just want you to locate him and then let me know where he is."

"You know, you are the second person who has wanted me to do this particular errand."

David Ramirez shook his head. "I know about that old man. Angela visited him at the retirement home. The children made his life less lonely. But he doesn't really care about Angela. Simon Delaney has something of his. I don't know what it is. I just know he wants to find Simon Delaney because he doesn't want me to find him first." Someone was clattering down the stairs. I could hear Bob the Fisherman's voice: He was making a run to the store. I eased around David Ramirez and went to the door of the shed. Bob the Fisherman had stopped in the doorway to the street and was kissing Toddy's caseworker. I turned back to my visitor.

"Did Simon shoot your daughter?"

Ramirez shrugged his shoulders. "I don't know for sure. That old man is crazy. But Simon Delaney was her husband. He should have stopped the whole thing. He should have helped her . . . but he didn't. How much does it cost for you to find him for me?"

I looked back out in the mudroom to make sure I wasn't hallucinating, but sure enough, Bob the Fisherman was pressing his face into the mouth of a representative of the State of Alaska's Department of Health and Social Services. I was dizzy with distraction as I turned back to Ramirez.

"Well, it all depends on how hard he is to find. I charge twenty-five dollars an hour. I might be able to locate him in an hour or a week. Can you come back tomorrow and tell me more about what you know about Delaney? Bring anything you can. Anything that has his name or any numbers . . . Social Security, things like that."

Ramirez began moving toward the door. He put his immense hands on my shoulders as he walked behind me and I suddenly felt like a child being ushered out of the principal's office.

Ramirez stepped into the mudroom and the couple broke their clench. Bob the Fisherman straightened his ratty beret and the caseworker smoothed down her pale blue blouse and licked her lips nervously, worrying about her smudged face. Ramirez smiled and ducked through the door. He turned back to me. "Tomorrow then" was all he said. Then he was out the door and gone.

Bob the Fisherman waved out into the rainy street. "Hey, Cecil, man," he said in a voice that was too loud for the situation, "I was just going to run for some . . . um . . . I was just going on a run for some . . ."

"Ice cream," the caseworker offered helpfully.

"Yeah, right. Ice cream," Bob said, teetering self-consciously on the balls of his feet, anxious to leave.

He went on, "Yeah. I'll be back in just a minute. You want anything from the store, baby?" He looked at the caseworker.

She flinched as if she were being spattered with animal blood. This may have been the first time in her adult life she had been called "baby" and I think she was just beginning to realize the depth of her mistake in kissing Bob the Fisherman.

"No," she gasped. "No . . . but thank you," and she turned away even before he walked out the door into the rain without another word.

"Well . . ." she said, straightening out her already straight blouse. "This is rather, well, you know, embarrassing." She laughed weakly and rubbed her index finger across her teeth, probably fearing she had lipstick smeared there.

"Aw, don't worry about it, Lois," I told her as I leaned close to pull a stray hair off the shoulder of the restraightened blouse. "Lots of people have put their tongue in Bob's mouth. I wouldn't worry about it."

"Well . . . whatever." She looked around, hoping, I suppose, there would be a trapdoor somewhere under her feet. "It's a good thing I bumped into you, actually," she said in a breezy voice, looking at me with an opaque professional air. "I have to talk to you about Todd."

"Do we have to talk about it now?" I glanced up the stairs, where I could hear the pounding feet that were starting the "Bunny Hop" chain around the room.

"Actually, Cecil, I just want to give you fair warning. We're concerned about Todd losing this last job. Not because of the job itself, frankly, but more because of the hole it leaves in his case plan."

"Hole?" I asked limply, not really wanting to have this conversation.

"That's right, hole. The job filled his case file and was good for his self-esteem. We need to fill that hole. We can't just have him, what, free-associating and giving his more obsessive behaviors a chance to take root. He needs work to keep him engaged with reality or you know what will happen, Cecil."

"Yeah, I know," I said, and tried to ease around her to the stairs.

"That's right. Without the engagement in the workplace he is liable to let his imaginative and, frankly, compulsive behavior come to the surface."

Todd used to talk to his dead mother. He had watched her die of hypothermia, and I suppose he felt guilty, but he never mentioned that. He simply wanted to know what heaven was like. He was never unreasonable about this and was never angry or frustrated concerning his mother's death, but the Department of Social Services apparently didn't like the fact that he wouldn't let his mother leave this earth completely.

"I just wanted to let you know this, Cecil, because we want you to keep Toddy busy. If he doesn't have a job, he has to be involved in a program. We don't want him just . . . you know . . . staring off into space."

"All right. No problem. We can keep him busy." I walked around her, then thinking of something else, I turned quickly and we bumped into each other on the stairs.

"Hey, Lois. You know Angela Ramirez?"

She had been caught by surprise and she found her hand resting on the front of my chest as if to push me away, but she didn't push. "Uh, yes. I knew Angela." She stepped back down one of the stairs but she let her hand linger on my chest. "Why? Did you know her, Cecil?" There was a crack in her voice.

"I knew her kids. They played around here. How are they?"

Lois took her hand down and flicked her finger nervously through her hair. "They're doing okay. As well as could be expected, I suppose. They're with some temporary foster parents. We're trying to locate the husband. He's the adoptive father and he left town several days before . . . the death." Lois nodded to the front door through which

Bob the Fisherman and David Ramirez had disappeared. "That was their grandfather, wasn't it? He spent the morning with the kids. He wants to take them back with him, I take it?"

I smiled. "I dunno. They didn't come up." I stared at her and she let her face fall into an opaque bureaucratic mask. I knew I wasn't going to get anything by fishing around with small talk. "Listen, Lois, can I talk to Angela's kids? I just have to ask them a couple of questions."

She walked past me on the stairs, speaking over her shoulder.

"Cecil, you know I can't let you talk to them. Simon Delaney is their legal guardian. You would need permission from him. I wouldn't worry about them. Simon Delaney will show up for those kids. And then you can deal with him." She continued on up the stairs. A chorus of voices was screeching out the bridge section to "Twist and Shout." She raised her voice above the bad harmonies. "But listen, Cecil, if I were you I'd be more concerned about Toddy. I'm not kidding. If you can't provide a good environment with economic stability, I'm afraid we're going to have to find another place for him." She turned and stood above me, gesturing with her open arms as if she were Eva Perón. "I know you two are close, but sometimes that closeness doesn't inform the best of judgments." She paused, pleased, I think, with her turn of a phrase. Then she went on. "Why do you want to talk to the kids, anyway?"

"I want to ask about what happened the day their mom died."

"The police have been over all that with them. Their mom had been drinking. She hit them. She went to the hotel and she . . ." The image of the killing passed across her expression. "She was killed. The kids don't want to talk about it anymore. Why would you want to pester them?"

"Because I think Simon Delaney knows who killed

their mom." I said it more just to try the words out rather than from any real conviction that they might be true.

The caseworker looked at me with an expression of pure befuddlement. She drew breath to set me straight when Bob the Fisherman burst through the door with a grocery bag of ice cream cartons, tortilla chips, and several ropes of red licorice.

"Hey, sugarlumps!" he called up to her in a thick romantic baritone. "You miss me?"

Lois dropped her arms to her sides. Wincing again, she looked as if she had just been reminded that she had rabies.

"Desperately," she said weakly, and turned to walk up the stairs alone.

Chapter Three

In the morning my house looked like the battlefield where the revolution had turned into a cocktail party. Pirate Ron was sleeping on the floor when I walked out into the kitchen. His bulk looked like a storm-tossed island lying on the linoleum: His stomach heaved up in the air and his face was hidden under a book of poetry perched over his face like the ridge of a tiny house inexplicably blown there. Balloons that had already shriveled into rotten fruit bumped along the floor, and streamers swung eerily in the pasty light of this new and promising day.

The phone rang. Somewhere. I dug around in the sofa cushions and found a remote for the TV and a paper plate covered with dog hair and icing, but no phone. Finally I grabbed the phone next to the stove.

"I say fuck the psychiatric bullshit. I want you to find Simon Delaney." Dickie's voice cut through the line like a chain saw.

"Good morning, Counselor," I said as I yawned.

"Yeah. Yeah, good morning. Listen, Cecil. I've been over what the doctor tells me. There is no way in hell this old guy is incompetent. He's just bullshitting you and that pencil-neck. Find that fucking Delaney before the cops do, goddamnit. I'm coming over later." The receiver went dead.

"Bye, bye," I said to the receiver as I put it back in the cradle.

Wendall, Todd's dog, was sleeping next to Ron on someone's expensive coat. He had half a leather shoe in his mouth. Wendall, that is. His breathing was louder than Pirate Ron's but it was a close contest. I stepped over them and put on the kettle to make coffee. I heard someone snuffling and as I turned, Ron rolled over on the floor putting his arm around Wendall, whose eyes opened only briefly. Todd was sitting on the couch in the same clothes he had worn for the party. They were wrinkled and his face had the red track of the arm of the couch, where he had apparently slept. He was thumbing through the new dictionary he had received for his birthday. He stared at me as if we had been in the middle of a conversation all through the night.

"Cecil," he said, his voice croaky with sleep, "I was thinking that perhaps I could trace my employment problems to a fundamental deficit in my vocabulary."

I stood by the teakettle with my hand on the handle but not watching it in accordance with the "watched pot" rule. "What are you talking about, Todd?"

"My employer said I was talking too much to the customers. But of course I have to communicate with them if I am to understand what they desire. I must have been using the wrong kind of language. I must have inadvertently been miscommunicating both with the customers and with my supervisors. So, I believe that if I increased my word power I could avoid these problems in the future."

The teakettle began a low rumble. I could feel it shimmy slightly under my hand. "I dunno. I think you know plenty of words, Todd. Maybe you should think about diction."

Todd's eyes brightened. He started flipping through the book mumbling to himself, "Diction. Diction . . . let's see . . . 'dictator' . . . 'diction: (1) manner of expression in words; choice of words. (2) enunciation.' "

He shook his head, puzzled. "Is that kind of like context, Cecil?"

"Shit, I don't know, Todd." Here Pirate Ron began to stir. He rolled onto his back and flipped the heavy book aside.

"Has it happened yet?" he demanded. His voice rumbled like the grinding continental plates. "The surge of weirdness. Has it happened?"

Wendall woke and took the leather shoe off to his own corner. I leaned over Pirate Ron and spoke into his half-closed eyes. "We're riding it out, brother. Don't move until the coffee is ready," I reassured him.

Toddy was back to his dictionary, mumbling the word "context" to himself.

Pirate Ron was breathing heavily. Then he blurted out, " 'O indigence at the root of our lives, how poor is the language of happiness!' "

I was spooning coffee into a filter as the kettle started rocking on the grate. I turned to Ron on the floor and spilled some of the grounds on the counter. "I know that from somewhere. Where'd you hear it?"

"I read it in your goddamn poetry book," he belched. "Why do you read that Commie shit?"

" 'Context' . . . 'context' . . . no . . . 'contention' . . . 'contest' . . ." Toddy intoned.

I leaned over Pirate Ron and stared down into the broken blood vessels of his eyes. "Whattaya mean, Commie shit? That quote is from a guy who died in one of Stalin's prison camps." The teakettle whistled.

"Exactly."

Todd placed his index finger in the book. "Here. 'Context: the parts just before and after a word or passage that determine its meaning.' "

Pirate Ron rolled up to the sitting position. Here, for some reason, he looked as if he had just fallen off a horse. He rubbed his head. "I'm sorry, man. It's happening. It's happening, isn't it? The weirdness surge."

"I'm lost," said Todd. "I might be able to know what came before, but I'll never be able to know what comes after until after it's already there. I'm really lost, Cecil."

Todd looked up from the dictionary and his head wobbled on his neck as if his thoughts were bocce balls rolling around in his skull.

"Me too," I said finally. "Let's have some breakfast." Then I poured three cups of coffee.

Jane Marie came out in her flannel nightgown. We drank coffee and juice, then had oatmeal with raisins. Pirate Ron looked at his watch and then flattened his hands against his cheeks as if conceptually washing his face.

"Oh, Christ. I've got to work today," he groaned.

I pulled on my slippers and poured a cup of coffee into a plastic cup. "I'll go with you," I said, and handed him one of the cups.

"Why?" Ron asked, as he took the coffee and headed to the door.

"I've got to find a guy. I think your foreman may know him."

"Jesus," he grunted, "you working, Younger?"

"Yeah. What's so odd about that?"

"I just thought you were a member of the leisure class. I didn't take you for actually having to work. Particularly the morning after a birthday ordeal."

"I know. I know. I was born to royalty but I live like this as a test of character until I reclaim my birthright," I said as we walked down the stairs to the street.

"Actually, I think you're just lazy," Ron's voice boomed in the narrow stairwell.

We walked outside, where, surprisingly, it wasn't raining. We pulled up the hoods of our raincoats just out of habit.

"Ah," he said, scanning the narrow street that had once been the main thoroughfare of the old Indian village after the Russians walled off the original encampment for their own. Otis was out on the pavement on his bicycle. He was wearing a conical party hat and was blowing a paper horn. Two ravens stood on the lip of the overflowing garbage cans. One had a piece of blue frosting on its beak, the other a loop of spaghetti. Ron slapped his chest with both hands and took in a deep breath of spring air.

"God, I love this life." He turned to me and stared down at me as if he were a biblical prophet. "Come, Younger, let us go to work and become useful." Then he strode away toward the humming machines of the fish plant. Otis honked his paper horn as we passed and the ravens took to the air.

The slime line at the fish plant is a stainless-steel-and-plastic sluice where the fishworkers clean and prepare the fish for whatever market they are intended for. The plant is built on a bulkhead next to the channel. Fishing boats are unloaded and the fish are brought in bins to the concrete buildings where they are cut up and packaged fresh or frozen for shipment.

The concrete hall reverberated with contemporary dance music. The room was cold and filled with the icy smell of fish. Young people stood in rain gear on each side of the table and danced with sharp knives. They were slicing fillets off of halibut. An older man walked behind them, occasionally speaking to them, offering encouragement or giving directions. The synthesized music throbbed, the melody completely subservient to the beat. The workers bobbed their heads up and down as their heavy rubber gloves worked quickly over the white flesh. Older women took the fillets, and the skeletons of halibut slid down a ramp to the meal grinder. I could see there was a rubber pad on the concrete floor where the workers stood. They shifted their feet in time to the music that swirled off the concrete walls and mixed easily with the industrial clatter of the plant.

"Oh, great. A half hour more of rave. I can't stand this shit." Pirate Ron pulled off his jacket and started getting into his coveralls. I knew the scene here. This shift had worked out a schedule for the music: The white college kids on the crew got a half hour of rave dance music. This was the dance throb they were working to now. Then there could be fifteen minutes of metal: Pearl Jam. Nirvana. Then fifteen minutes of rap. This had been cut back from a half hour when one of the supervisors actually heard some of the lyrics. The rap fans were teenage white boys with close-cropped blond hair and tattered skateboard T-shirts. One of them had argued persuasively for a rap slot and he tried to spin a selection that had less of the hard-core gangsta sound. Then there was an hour of middle-of-the-road rock: Springsteen, Bob Seger. Then a half hour of contemporary country. There were Filipino and Samoan workers, a couple of Africans, and several white college kids, all in their twenties. There had been several serious arguments about music, a couple of fights, and one "accidental" stabbing. The music agreement had to be worked out with the foreman. They did this to avoid conflict on the shifts. Giving them a choice in the music seemed to keep them happy and working hard. After all, the rhythm was fast and steady; good for fast repetitive work.

Pirate Ron was approaching fifty. He had been in Vietnam, and secretly he liked chamber music, but at work he made the young crew listen to the Plasmatics and the Sex Pistols. They didn't care. They just kept working as long as Ron didn't hassle them about the tunes they chose. Once Ron put on an old field recording of chain gang work songs, but

all the young kids on the crew made him turn it off. The beat
was too slow.

The foreman saw me and agreed to talk for a couple
of minutes in his office. As he shut the door, the noise fell
away as if we had gone up in a hot air balloon.

I knew the foreman from the neighborhood. His
name was Louis Tom. His grandma was one of the powerful
elders of his clan. I had been friends with his brother who
had taught Tlingit language and traditions in the jails. Louis
kicked back in his chair and put his rubber boots up on the
dented metal desk.

"To what do I owe the pleasure?" he said with a sour
expression.

"I'm looking for Simon Delaney," I said, and Louis
immediately grimaced.

"Simon. Oh, man, I don't know." He twisted around
in his chair and looked at the calendar that was taped to the
wall behind him.

"I think he took off a couple of days before . . . that
deal with his wife." He turned back toward me. "That was
too bad, huh?"

I couldn't think how to answer for a moment. I
thought of the young woman with a large-caliber slug
through her skull. I thought of the bloody water spilling out
of the bathtub.

"Yeah . . . it was too bad," I said. "He worked here
for a while, right?"

"Well . . ." Louis rubbed his chin, "in a manner of
speaking. He was an occasional. He worked here some. I
saw him mostly with that big guy, Marcus. Did you know
him?"

I nodded. I had seen them both walking down the
street in front of my house. They were hard to miss. Marcus
looked to be close to six and a half feet tall. He could have
been a Pacific islander, with some heritage tracing back to

Africa. A broad torso, wide face, and tight curly hair. Simon was a dark-haired terrier with a crooked nose and a slight limp.

"I'd seen them around," I offered.

Louis nodded and looked around his desk as if his memory might be there. "Marcus showed up along with Simon but he didn't get on the crew. Marcus mostly hung around in the break room. He did a few days' work but mostly he was talking to the crew. Some of the guys wanted me to throw him out but, man, he was large, you know what I mean? I told them to throw him out if they wanted."

"What did Marcus do in the break room?"

Louis stopped scanning his desk. "Well, it was like he was organizing a union but he didn't have any real organization. He just called it 'consciousness raising' . . . but I didn't really follow it. But he never talked to me."

"How did Simon do on the crew?" I asked as I fished into my pocket for something to write with.

"I liked Simon okay. He worked hard. He was political too, but not so much like Marcus. He just used to ask if I was happy all the time."

"If you were *happy*?" I found the pencil stub but no paper.

"Yeah. He would act concerned, and just out of the blue ask if I were happy. He asked everybody that. Then they would start talking about their family and their job. Simon would get them talking about things and then Marcus would meet them after work. I think they had it planned that way."

I could hear the thump of bass and the muffled rumble of angry black males as the quarter hour of rap started on the slime line. "Was Simon into drugs?" I raised my voice to ask.

Louis shook his head and looked at his clipboard. "Not that I know of, Cecil. Simon was a drinker on and off.

He acted almost like a religious nut, but I never heard him talk about Jesus or anything. He just asked people if they were happy, and if they said they were, he asked them why and if it would last. I had one guy complain about him. Some people thought he was gay. But, shit . . ." Louis shrugged his shoulders, "there's nothing I could do about that. You know?"

I nodded my head in agreement. "Did he leave any papers or application forms?" I gave up on the idea of writing anything down for myself.

Louis was still looking in his papers on the clipboard. "Yeah. Let me find the date he filled it out." He kicked back in his chair and expertly rolled in front of his green metal file cabinet. He opened the bottom drawer and thumbed through the files. His finger came to a stop and he pulled out a file and scooted toward me.

"I did know his wife," Louis said as he scanned the clipboard. "Angela didn't much like it here. She was having a hard time staying sober. I saw her once at a meeting, you know. She was working her program. Simon said he would leave her if she fell off. But he's the one, man. He was shit-faced before he left town. Yeah, I got it," and he swung around in his chair and started to hand a file to me, then pulled back. "It's okay for me to give this stuff to you, isn't it?"

I reached across for the file, smiling, with my voice calm and confident. "I'm certain there's no problem with me asking for these files, legally, if that's what you mean?"

For just a moment he held on to the file and I tugged gently. "Listen, Louis. Go ahead and check with your boss."

He let go and wheeled back behind the desk. "Aw, the heck with it. Just don't take it anywhere. Okay?"

"Of course." I grinned and spread the file open on my knees.

I found an old receipt in my pants pocket and I

wrote Simon Lee Delaney's Social Security number on it. His birthday. He was thirty-seven years old. He had been born in Centralia, Washington. On the application form where he had to list contacts for medical emergencies he listed: *William Flynn, Uncle, Sitka, Alaska*, with the Pioneers' Retirement Home telephone number. On the second line he had: *Bill Haywood, Dutch Harbor... Advisor.* There was a 581 telephone number listed, and I copied it down.

Under religion he had written "None" and then he had scratched it out and written in block letters: "ANARCHIST."

"I know he loved her." Louis's voice cut through my thoughts.

"Huh?" I asked.

"Simon Delaney. He loved his wife." Louis was pointing at the papers in my hand as if that would illustrate what he was talking about. "He bought her presents and stuff. He would brag about her. How pretty she was. It was odd too, because he used to brag about how poor she had been. How hard it was for Mexican-Americans. It was like he was proud of that part too."

"What was Delaney?" I squinted at Louis, trying to remember the looks of the man I'd seen walking down my street.

"Delaney said he was pure working-class from the Pacific Northwest: part Chinese, part Swedish, and part Irish. His daddy had been in the IRA, he said. But who knows if *that* was true."

I gave Louis back his file and let him get back to work. I walked past the slime line. Pirate Ron was cleaning a stainless steel grate with a pressure hose. The rest of the crew were hustling to clean fish for the restaurants of Seattle and San Francisco. The white skate punks were bobbing and working efficiently as Public Enemy's song, "Fight The Power," careened off the concrete walls. Ron had his earplugs in, but he waved as he saw me headed for the door. He held his gloved hands out to his side and made a goofy confused face. "It's happening, man. It's happening, I'm telling you." I waved back as I stepped out onto the street where it was just starting to rain.

There was a note on my door from Mr. Ramirez. It was one line and said simply: *Not going to need you. David Ramirez.*

I walked upstairs where Toddy was still picking up the paper plates and beer bottles that were tucked behind the couch in the corner. I think our guests thought the garbage would just biodegrade there. I went to the kitchen phone and dialed the Dutch Harbor number Simon Delaney had listed on his application form. The phone rang five times and I was about to hang up when a very deep male voice answered.

"Bill's Round Ball."

I cleared my throat and spoke in a higher register. "Yeah. This is Richard Face from Alaska Express. I've got a package here for Simon Delaney. The package has this number. Is that right?"

"Whatever you say. You want Simon?" The deep voice sounded sleepy.

"No, that's all right. I just have to confirm the address. It got smeared in the rain, you know. It's a package from Centralia, Washington. Does that sound right?"

"Hell, I don't know, man. Let me get Simon."

"No, really, that's all right. I'll just send it along to—what? Bill's . . . I can't make it out."

"Yeah. Yeah. Wild Bill's Round Ball Roundup, Box six-eight-seven, Unalaska." I heard pounding resonating in the background. The speaker was losing his patience but I needed to push a little harder.

"Physical address?" I sputtered out as if I were working down a short checklist.

"The old skating rink. Right downtown. Can't miss it."

"Aaaand Mr. Delaney will be around in the next couple of days to sign for it?" I chirped in my best "this-is-no-big-deal,-I'm-just-winding-this-up" tone of voice. I had my eyes closed. I was barely breathing.

"He better be, goddamnit. He's supposed to work for me."

"Allllrighty then. Thanks. Bye-bye." I hung up the phone as if it were radioactive.

Dickie Stein poked his head over the stair rail. He looked at his watch and then at me.

"What the hell are you still doing here? I thought I told you to find Delaney."

"And good morning to you, Counselor." I spread my arms wide to the disaster of my home. "Have you checked the balance on your medication lately? You seem to have a little edge on."

He stomped around the stairs. Dickie had graduated from Harvard Law when he was nineteen and it had stunted his development. He was stuck in some type of adolescent rage fueled by an IQ of 150. Today he was wearing baggy shorts and had his red rubber boots rolled down to midcalf. He wore a Sid Vicious T-shirt and his own hair had a kind of dirty-hair-horn, fuck-the-police look to it. He had a manila envelope under his arm, and lawyerly wire-rimmed glasses on. He looked around at the distressed room, then sat down quickly in the only clear space on the sofa. I perched on a block of wood next to the stove. Toddy was in the corner on his hands and knees picking up bits of wrapping paper the kids had turned into confetti. Dickie smiled over at Todd and then looked at me as if I were a rodent.

He threw the manila envelope on the table. "There's two thousand dollars in there. You can use it how you like. Just find fucking Simon Delaney, would you?"

I lifted the package and sampled the heft. The envelope was as thick as a peanut butter sandwich. "Has Mr. Flynn talked with Angela's father about any of this?"

He flinched. Dickie was a pitiful poker player. He loved fucking with people so much it hindered him as a lawyer.

"I wouldn't know anything about that." He was looking at the manila envelope in my hand. "William Flynn wants to locate Simon Delaney. He says Delaney will lead you to Ole Hanson. I personally don't give a shit about whoever this Hanson is—I just want Delaney."

"Let me just ask theoretically, will I get more money if Simon Delaney has an accidental death?"

"Jesus," Dickie said. "Cecil, you watch too much television."

Back behind me I heard the teakettle whistle, and Toddy stood up from his position on the floor and padded over to the stove. I leaned across to Dickie.

"Simon Delaney has something on William Flynn. The old boy wants Delaney dead," I said to my lawyer.

"Flynn has said nothing about killing Delaney. You do not have to be concerned about that." Dickie was speaking to me but couldn't seem to take his eyes off the envelope of money.

I put down the envelope and watched his eyes follow it as I spoke to him. "The truth is, I need more money, particularly if I'm going to be taking a trip to felonyland."

No one spoke. Todd stirred honey into his tea. Outside the gulls were playing their ragged whistles and a troller was blowing the carbon out of its exhaust.

Finally, Dickie shrugged and stood up. "Let's go talk to him about it." He walked down the stairs. I picked up the money and followed.

In a few minutes we were in William Flynn's room at the Pioneers' Home. The windows were open and the dead flowers had been taken out. Flynn sat in his wheelchair and didn't speak as I laid it out for him just as I had for the lawyer. Finally I put the unopened manila envelope in his lap. He didn't speak. He stared without recognition at the packet and I could hear the air working its way in and out of his leathery old flesh. Then he looked up at me and spoke in a voice that was weaker since yesterday.

"Ramirez was here. Today. He knows that Simon is in Dutch Harbor."

Outside the window a tiny finch flitted onto the thin branches of a wild apple tree in the garden.

I took a patient breath. Being conditioned to respect my elders, I tried to choose my words carefully but in this case there was nothing to do but to plow ahead like a tug. "Here's what I think. You are going to be tried and convicted of killing Angela Ramirez. The doctor is all optimistic that you are not going to be found competent to stand trial. But I am not. There are people a hell of a lot crazier than you serving time. And your age isn't going to help buy you a lot of sympathy. You are what they call a cheap life sentence. The DAs get a first-degree conviction and you are only going to take up bed space for a year or two, tops. They love that. So listen, old man, you are going down for this murder." The old man shot a look at me and then bit his tongue. "This isn't about finding a quiet place to be buried. This is about who shot Angela Ramirez. Now, let's for the sake of argument say that Simon Delaney knows that you did it. Let's say Delaney turns out to be a witness against you. Why in the hell should you want me to find him? And remember this clearly: I am not killing him for you."

William's shaky hand wiped his mouth and he stared out past the finch, past the mountains and the water which was being stirred by a faint wind from the southeast. He was staring a long, long way into the distance. His voice was thin and reedy:

"We never planned to leave our homestead. When we came to town it was just so Tommy could see the doctor. We ended up never going back. It's all still there, as far as I know. All set and ready for us."

He kept looking out the window. The limbs of the wild apple etched in the reflection on the glass cast a slight shadow over his face.

"We'll never go back, will we?" He stared at me briefly then turned back to the window. "Tommy used to string the radio antenna up in the tree. He listened to the Giants. They were the first team to give a black man a break, you know?" He fumbled in the pockets of his baggy pants for a red bandanna. "I told him it was foolish to climb that damn tree. One winter he fell from the very top branch. Almost broke his fool neck," William said, then blew his nose.

"All I can seem to do these days is think about all the stupid things we've done . . . for good reasons." William's eyes were closed. I thought he was dozing off.

"They called it a massacre," he murmured. I leaned forward and touched his arm and the old man opened his eyes suddenly.

"I had a friend when I was a boy. Ole Hanson. Did I tell you about him? I want you to find him. I want to be buried next to him. That's all I want."

"Is Ole Hanson dead already?" Dickie asked.

William bit his lip and turned away from the window. The wheel of his chair in the cramped quarters knocked his bedside table: Pills spilled out on the table next to the alarm clock and his barlow knife under the reading lamp. William looked at the pills with disgust. "Yes. I think Ole is dead. But I don't know for sure. That's what they say, but I don't know for sure. Just find Simon Delaney. He knows."

The old man turned to me and his head was not shaking and his gaze was steady, fierce. "I don't give a damn what Simon Delaney says about Angela or about how she died. He knows where Ole Hanson is and I want you to find him." William rocked in his chair. He shoved the envelope of money at me. Suddenly, the tears were rolling again.

"What about your brother? Wouldn't you like to be near your brother when you die?" Dickie asked.

William sat up urgently and said unequivocally, "Ole Hanson is *not* my brother!" Then he slumped back down into the chair.

"I never wanted those boys to die." He was crying as he said this. He took my hand.

"Simon Delaney can find Ole Hanson. I'm sure of it. Get to Simon before Angela's father does. Get to Simon only because he knows where Ole is. I need to be with him, you understand? Ole Hanson." The old man's grip was surprisingly strong, but his skin was growing pale, his breathing shallow.

"Go to the cabin on the homestead. You can have it all." He was gasping now. Dickie was calling down the hall for the nurse. "These goddamn lawyers. They just screw it up." Sweat was beading on his forehead but his hand was cold, as if the old man were turning to stone. "To hell with Simon Delaney. He can tell the world if he likes. It does not matter now." Then William closed his eyes. As I put his hand down on the chair I was elbowed out of the way by an orderly and a nurse.

They wheeled him down to the clinic room near the nurses' station and I overheard one of the nurses ask for the doctor on call. I walked down the stairwell ahead of my lawyer.

"This is bullshit," I told Dickie, and I was embarrassed by the way the word echoed in the concrete stairwell. "Let's just bury him next to Tommy and give his money to Angela's kids." I remembered the envelope with the two thousand dollars. "Well . . . most of the money. I mean, there will be expenses," I added before the echo had faded.

"I have to admit I think that's probably the best idea," Dickie said. "I don't think we have much time to work his case. Let's face it, Cecil, he's going to be dead soon . . . . I mean I can drag this case on long enough they'll never get a chance to convict him." His voice trailed off and he looked up at me for reassurance that we weren't converting our client into carrion. But I couldn't look at him. We stepped out onto the porch and he nervously went back to William's file.

"I was just going through here, looking . . ."

The midmorning jet was taking off across the channel. Down the street some of the early season tourists were bumbling across the street trying to take pictures of the Russian Cathedral, and Alice was standing in her gray coat feeding the pigeons. The birds were scrambling for the crumbs sprinkled on the concrete. I watched as a fat raven waddled arrogantly into the crowd of plump gray birds. I looked carefully and smiled as I recognized that the raven had a red thread looped around his right leg. The lawyer kept rustling his papers.

"Cecil," he said, as I kept watching the raven and thinking about where I had seen that red thread before.

"Cecil!" he said, more urgently. "I don't think we know where Tommy is buried."

"What do you mean?" I said, barely listening, but watching the pigeons clear the way for the greedy raven to eat the crumbs.

"I mean Tommy Flynn left the home. He checked out with one of his relatives."

Alice tossed down an entire slice of dry toast and the birds cleared away. The raven grabbed the slice and lumbered into the air. He flew over the lip of the porch and I could hear his black feathers working against the air.

I didn't really want to think about the answer to my next question so I watched the tenuous red thread on the raven's leg disappear before I asked, "Who was the relative?"

Dickie flopped down on the steps and looked out to sea. "Tommy Flynn signed out of here in May of 1986. Under his own steam and in the company of Simon Delaney."

"Yeah." I sat next to my lawyer. "That just about makes sense," I said as a piece of toast fell out of the sky like a cartoon anvil at our feet.

Chapter Four

Even if the facts are bad for your client, it's better to find out sooner rather than later, say, in the middle of trial. I wasn't so worried that William Flynn may have killed Angela but I hated thinking there was someone out there who might have known more about the killing than I did. That was in effect what David Ramirez had told me and what Dickie and I had a vague sense of: Delaney knew. And in a murder trial, knowledge, even guilty knowledge — *especially* guilty knowledge — is the coin of the realm.

I had missed the day flight to Juneau. It was my only connection to Anchorage and the early morning flight to Dutch Harbor. David Ramirez had probably made the afternoon flight, so there was no earthly way I could beat him to Dutch Harbor and Simon Delaney.

I had enough money from William Flynn's envelope to charter a small prop plane to Juneau. But I needed more and I thought I knew where I could come by it. With the two thousand I could pay for an extra landing and stop at the Flynn brothers' old cabin at Stormy Reach. According to the doctor, the brothers brought very little gear with them when they'd checked into the home. There were no receipts for the storage bins which usually accompany people who pare down their belongings to come to their final address. I figured Tommy Flynn must have headed back to his homestead after he walked out of the home with Simon in 1986.

Jane Marie was packing for a trip to Frederick Sound. She was going in her own boat, the *Winning Hand*, off for ten days to see if the humpback whales were starting to congregate on the feeding grounds there. She only barely acknowledged my explanation that I was going to be gone for a while. She thought Toddy could fend for himself and was pretty sure Priscilla and Young Bob could stay at the house with him if there were any problems. I packed my old Forest Service day pack, then ate a paper bowlful of cold spaghetti and freezer-burned halibut as I walked down the street to the float plane dock.

I walked past the fishermen's supply store and the accountant's office. Up the dock a little girl was posing for a picture, standing next to a bloody shark hanging from a steel cable hooked to a crane. It was a salmon shark, dull gray with the knifelike vertical tail fin and pale black spots on its belly. It looked perhaps six feet long and the eyes were black as deep holes. The girl shrieked and stepped back as some of the shark's blood dripped on her clean tennis shoes. I walked past and missed the story of catching the shark, the story being the only usable thing about shark fishing, in my opinion.

The flight over was smooth. The islands to the north of Sitka are steep rocky patches topped with spruce and hemlock trees. As we took off from the busy channel I looked down: The tide was low and many of the shallow rocks were exposed, looking like elephants garlanded with kelp standing up from their wallow. The air and the water were calm. The waves broke barely white on the black volcanic shoreline. To the west, sea lions were hauled out on the bare rocks. Gulls scattered like seeds below the blare of the plane's engine.

Flying usually induces a mild form of hysteria in me. But the sky and sea seemed so benign on this particular day I was able to keep my eyes mostly open and my hands cramped only slightly as I gripped the seat. I sat next to the pilot, watching all the incomprehensible dials and gauges and thinking that it didn't really look so hard, this flying business, once one learned to read these damn numbers.

After about an hour, the plane banked over a rocky inlet and circled up against the side of the mountain. Below the right wing the trees rushed by, but not so fast that I couldn't make out the needles on their boughs or the sticky pods that would later become cones. The plane leveled out and gently touched down on the water. The floats bounced only slightly as we eased in. The engine backed off, then built again to push the plane on top of the water. A tiny dock was anchored near the shore and a log with broken planking hung from the bank to the dock. While he tied the plane to some rusty cleats, the pilot agreed to wait half an hour. I worked my way up the decking to the shore on my hands and knees, not knowing if the rotten wood would handle my weight.

This was Stormy Reach. The cabin sat inside the anchorage of a small island off the coast of Chichagof Island. At the mouth of the anchorage was a shallow reef that a large boat would have to judge warily before crossing at a mid- to high tide. The crossing could not be done by any boat at low tide when the reef broke and blocked the anchorage. Even on a day as calm as this one, the swells sucked around the rocks and the green water broke white. Standing at the top of the ramp I could not see the ocean through the trees but I could hear the swells breaking. The wind pouring around me was damp and salty. There were no other sounds or smells in this forested seascape and I stood there for a moment with an empty mind until the scream of an oystercatcher cut through. The black bird with a long red beak was flitting around the rocks near the low tide line. I shook my head as if waking up, then started down the overgrown trail to the cabin site.

William and Tommy Flynn's cabin was intact but the cedar walls had been so weathered by the rains and wind they were almost black as char. The cabin was maybe sixteen by twenty with a peaked metal roof and windows only in the front and the back. As I came closer I stepped across a fallen fence: rotted wooden posts and galvanized wire mesh. Stepping over the mesh I noticed the outline of what had been a garden spot. Mounds of earth under thick tangles of chickweed and salmonberry brambles. There were tripods set at the ends of some of the rows but the string hanging between them was tangled in the weeds. The gate was still standing but I had walked right by it. Near the gate was the rusted head of a shovel, and a pair of rotted leather gloves was dissolving into the top of the slick mildewed post.

The front door of the cabin had a hasp that had been broken away years ago. The door was shut but as I eased against it one of the hinges gave way from the rotten wood.

The air inside the cabin was close with mildew and diesel fuel. There were two iron cots in each far corner and an oil heater in the middle. Near the front door was a wood cookstove and a small wooden table with two chairs near the only window in front. There was a kerosene lamp on the table and a candle in a fruit jar sitting on the windowsill. I found a sealed jar with some wax-covered wooden matches inside. After trying a few of the matches one sparked and I lit the candle in the jar. I couldn't see any trunks or storage bins in the dark corners of the cabin. The beds had mattresses that were rolled up on the wire webbing. I unrolled one of the mattresses and found nothing but a ragged hole where the stuffing was tufted out and a collection of mouse droppings. In the opposite corner from the table was a pile of rotted beets. The head and spine of a deer hung from a rafter. Maggots rolled down from the strands of flesh around the vertebrae. Some hunter, most likely a poacher, had used this corner of the cabin to bone out his buck.

The wood stove was empty except for some wet sticks and burnt matches from when someone had tried and failed to build a fire. I looked into the kindling box and saw only a pile of mildewed *Soviet Life* magazines. Flipping through the musty pages I watched images jitter by: new tractors, combines in fields of winter wheat, pink-cheeked girls hefting boxes onto flatbed trucks, cosmonauts and giant dams, fishermen and uniformed soldiers. All in large-format color shots soaked through with light but hazy now with mildew.

Above the table at eye level, photographs and notes were tacked to the plywood wall. The photographs were curled with age and represented different eras of people who had stood in the flower garden outside: A black-and-white print showed a somber woman next to the black-eyed Susans; a color snapshot showed a girl with a bouffant hairdo and harlequin eyeglasses leaning into the stalks of some vivid gladiolus; there was a clear color print of a man with a ponytail and a beard holding a baby and a spray of shasta daisies.

There was a note in pencil, blotched and almost unreadable: POTASH, VINEGAR, WHITE GAS.——DON'T FORGET YOUR PILLS.

Below as if in answer: *I'll be down at the creek for one last look around. Don't forget to bring back that fencing for the far corner.*

Something cracked against the metal roof and I walked outside. It had sounded like someone throwing stones but there was no one, and I could see my pilot's feet sticking out of the passenger side of the plane. He was apparently taking a quick nap. Then I saw a crow under the eaves fly up with what looked like a mussel shell in his beak. He circled up over my head and then over the cabin, where he dropped the shell on the metal roof. The mussel clattered down and fell off the eave unbroken. Now the crow flew to the mussel and took it up higher and dropped it against the stone wall of a root cellar. This time it broke and the crow dove down and gobbled the rubbery flesh inside. He waddled proudly along the frame of the root cellar door as I came close. He rattled at me as I lifted the door open. As I walked down into the cellar with the candle, the crow took to the air.

There were racks on each side of the dark enclosure. Several burlap bags appeared to be filled with dirt but must have once contained potatoes or beets. The smell was sweet and sour with rot. There were a dozen cases of canning jars: canned beets and rutabagas, canned fish and venison. The rings were tight and the jars all had kept their seal. By the front door was a rusted commercial can of peaches and underneath that was a metal footlocker.

I lugged the footlocker out into the sunlight. It was covered in dirt and had a fine coating of mildew. When I tried to open the latches, the box would not open. A strange wax coated the seals, as if someone had preserved the contents with the same care as they had preserved the food. I could not open the locker until I ran the tip of my knife around the seams of the opening. The hinges gave way from the wax-coated fiberboard of the box as I opened it. The contents had been sealed away from the moisture so the papers inside were clean.

I was filled with the thrill of a natural voyeur. There were bundles of papers and photographs tied together with waxed cord. The photographs were square black-and-whites that must have been taken decades ago with an old-style box camera. The edges of the photos had been cut with pinking shears and several of them had paste and torn paper on their backs as if they had been carelessly taken from an album.

There was a young woman in a long black dress standing on the covered porch of a wood frame house, her hair tied carefully in a bun, her dress gathered at her throat in a stiff collar that was fixed with a carved bone pin. The young woman had a kindly expression but her eyes were cast down and her hands hung loosely at her sides as if she were helpless to stop the photographer from taking her picture.

Another showed two young men, perhaps twenty years old, wearing knickers, each standing with one foot on the bottom step of what could have been the same porch, squinting into the sun. They had their arms draped carelessly around each other's shoulders and each pulled at their short-billed caps as if they were saluting a pretty girl.

Another showed just the formal portrait of a stern man, possibly in his late fifties, with wire-rimmed glasses and a handlebar mustache. He had a high starched collar and his thumb looped in his vest; a heavy-looking watch chain ran across his ample belly.

Nothing was written on any of the photos. There were no names or dates or written descriptions. They were like unsigned notes in a bottle, fragments of a memory, separated from their story.

There was a well-worn leather case that had a fine brass clasp and loops so the pouch could be worn on a belt. I undid the clasp and the thick leather was still supple and strong. Inside was a thin red book labeled IWW. SONGS. There was the symbol of a globe and the words, "The Industrial Workers of the World." On the inside front cover of this pamphlet were the words of the preamble to the constitution of the IWW:

> The working class and the employing class have nothing in common. There can be no peace so long as hunger and want are found among millions of working people and the few, who make up the employing class, have all the good things of life.

Between these two classes a struggle must
go on until the workers of the world organize as a class, take possession of the earth and
the machinery of production, and abolish the
wage system.

There was a name written on the inside cover but it
had been crossed out several times with heavy black ink. The
songbook was sewn together and showed the wear of dark
thumbprints on the edges of all the pages. A slip of paper
marked the song "Rebel Girl" by Joe Hill. On the paper was
written:

Long before resources run out, the shit will
hit the fan. A management regime will over-
power the democratic rules of government.
The regime will be funded by profits stolen
from the workers. Its propaganda will tout
safety, order, and defense of the borders,
then it will increase taxes on wages (but not
profits) in order to pay for the occupying
security force and the cost of prisons. — Tom

The handwriting was an old-style cursive, and below
in another hand was written in plain block letters:

In this garden plot
we show only clear profit
the rest of our lives. — William

The handwriting was of the same two people who
had written the notes I'd found on the wall of the cabin.
Scraps of old conversations. I folded the paper back into the

songbook. At the bottom of the locker was a red felt pennant, with red ribbons at the corners. Next to the stamp of Industrial Workers of the World, in bold white letters, it read: ONE BIG UNION. Folded and wrapped inside the pennant were the yellowed pages of newspapers that were nearly as fragile as dried leaves. There was an article on women getting the vote and another on Prohibition. Underneath these were other articles which had been marked in black pencil.

The first was from the October 21, 1919 *Centralia Daily Chronicle*, under the headline: "IWW Problem Discussed: The Centralia Citizens Protective Association Completed Its Organization at Well-Attended Meeting Last Night in Elks Club—Demand Closing of Headquarters." The short article listed the names of the officers elected to meet the demands of the community to shut down the Industrial Workers of the World Hall.

The next paper was from the *Centralia Daily Chronicle* of November 22, 1919. Half the paper was torn away and only the left-hand side of the front page remained. Only one word of the top headline was left, the bold-lettered word FUGITIVES. Then under that in smaller type, the headline teaser read: "*Hanson and Davis may be captured today. One of the largest posses yet went out to round up those suspected of being connected with the Armistice Day massacre. The posse left this morning at six o'clock to cover the seven camps of the Thurston County Logging Company following the receipt of a verbal message from these camps to the effect that 'the men wanted' were there. The posse is composed of between seventy-five and one hundred men who are heavily armed and prepared for any resistance the suspects may show.*" The rest of the article was torn away.

The last slip of newsprint was dated five months later, May 20, 1920, from the *Montesano Vidette*. The very brief news blurb was circled in the same black pencil. "*The remains of a man who is suspected to have been Ole Hanson were found last Monday by a farmer some four miles northeast of Oakville and near the Union Timber Company. Although the remains were transported to Olympia for identification, there are no records of just who the dead man may have been."*

In the margin of the paper was an exclamation mark in the same black pencil and in the same cursive handwriting were written the words: WE DID IT!

The crow landed and walked across the top of the root cellar door. I could hear his feet scratch the wood. He poked his head quickly in one direction and then the other. He fixed on something behind me briefly, then flew.

"We've got to get out of here," the pilot's voice boomed as he walked the trail up from the plane.

I jumped up and instinctively jammed the papers back into the footlocker. As I did, my fingers grazed the corners of a tin box. It was black, with worn red and green paint. There was no recognizable design, but the tin reminded me of something for a Christmas cake. I opened it and found four stacks of bills. All of them hundreds. Original silver certificates.

"Sorry to rush you, but we've got to be going." The pilot's voice was close over my shoulder. I slammed the footlocker shut and hauled it back down into the cellar. Inside the cellar I slipped the square tin into my backpack. As I walked up out of the cellar the pilot was standing over me silhouetted by the sun.

"Yeah, I mean we better get going. I need to get you over to the airport in Juneau if you want to make the afternoon flight to Anchorage and Dutch Harbor."

I nodded to the pilot and followed him to the plane. As the engine blared and the floats of the plane rattled against the water I remembered a day, years ago in Sitka, when I ran into William Flynn and we walked together to the coffee shop. We passed the American Legion Hall on the left side of the street. There William stopped and stood erect, glaring at the front of the squat blue building. Inside were men, old friends of his probably, sitting in the dark and drinking. William spit on the door. "What the hell are you doing?" I remember asking him at the time. He stood and said nothing. Then his fists unclenched and the anger seemed to lift out of his body, leaving the old man teetering flatfooted on the sidewalk.

"Old, old, old business," was all he'd say, then turned and walked away.

Dutch Harbor is a fishing port and a body of water. Unalaska is the name of the town adjacent to it. Both are halfway down the Aleutian Chain, between the Bering Sea and the Gulf of Alaska. Unalaska is farther south than Ketchikan but so far west it pushes the time zone to the limit. Alaska happens to be the state in the union that is the farthest west and the farthest east. True fact. At one time I planned to make a fortune on bar bets with this information, but I never ended up drinking in bars that had accurate globes or atlases. The land mass of the Aleutians has more in common with the islands of Hawaii than it does with the islands of southeastern Alaska. The Aleutians are steep, with rugged headlands and half-moon sandy beaches carved into the basalt. There are no trees around Dutch Harbor, except for a couple in the city park, but the hills are grassy rounded humps that build to stone peaks. Many of the volcanoes are perfectly symmetrical, with very sharp cones, as if they were imagined by Dr. Seuss. In summer, which has no predictable beginning, the landscape turns emerald green and is scattered with wildflowers. In spring, the mountains are camel-colored. There are no mammals except blue foxes and ground squirrels. No bears, deer, or anything else that walks on legs. The town surrounding Dutch Harbor has the industrial feel of a bustling port: muddy pickup trucks and clattering lifts work to haul fish and cargo out of the ships.

The weather systems here are violent and the waves boil almost constantly against the islands. In Sitka we smell the Japanese current, but in the Aleutians the Siberian arctic weather slides over the top of the Asian currents and stirs everything into a stormy mess. The locals on the street will meet you and say, "Well, you're sure here for the good weather," while you're standing in what anyone else would call a storm. A good day is when it's not blowing forty knots. The biggest and the best-designed ships fish these waters and still they sink with surprising regularity.

Dutch Harbor is the busiest fishing port in America, both by weight and by value. It's a world away from anywhere else. Here workers can get rich or barely break even. In the late seventies during the great king crab seasons, many fortunes were made. Some of the money got invested in mutual funds and real estate adjoining golf courses, but even now many, many of the fortunes made in Dutch Harbor are drunk up in the bars and sucked through the nostrils of the workers willing to work in one of the most dangerous fisheries in the world.

It takes two hours nonstop jet time to get there from Anchorage. The weather is always rough, the runway is short, and many of the passengers are drunk; this all lends itself to a sort of catastrophic carnival atmosphere. I was prepared for this: I cadged away an old prescription of Xanax, and even though I had been clean for a while I sucked the pills down with a diet Coke in the lounge at the Anchorage airport. This should have been enough to put me out for most any rough flight, and, in fact, I was dozing nicely as the plane eased up over the Alaska peninsula, but as we skirted the Bering Sea the body of the plane started to shake. I opened my eyes dreamily and saw a camera case spill out of the overhead container. The flight attendant was balancing her way to the front of the plane carrying a wet towel and an airsickness bag. I heard a high hiccupping voice of a woman either crying or praying. I closed my eyes. I remember only a few other things. The fisherman across the row from me urinated in his vomit bag and handed it, with a crooked smile, to the attendant. A Japanese man in an expensive blue business suit got caught smoking in the bathroom. He came bouncing back to his seat with the flight attendants screaming at him about federal air regulations. He smiled and nodded, smiled and nodded. The dark-haired stewardess brushed her hair back quickly and gripped the creaking seats. Her voice was tight and starting to break. "Even if you don't know our language you still have to obey the law," she told him. Then she walked forward. The Japanese man gave her the finger as she passed. I closed my eyes and kept them closed as the plane dropped through the cloud cover and banked steeply against the side of the mountain. I kept them closed as the tires gripped the runway and I was thrown forward in my seat by the back-thrust of the engines. I opened them only after the plane pivoted at the end of the runway. I looked out the window and saw the spray from waves falling on the apron just yards from where the jet had stopped.

There was some holdup with getting the ramp of the plane down so I asked for a cup of coffee just to perk up. The flight attendants weren't mad at me because I'd slept most of the way, but I had the feeling they wanted the federal marshals to meet most of the rest of the passengers.

I was feeling almost perky by the time I stepped out on the runway. Walking across to the terminal, I looked at the tan grassy hills and took a deep breath. I had the feeling of being a long way from home.

Inside the cramped terminal building, families were embracing and businessmen were shaking hands. The Japanese smoker was bowing to two other men with white hard hats and clipboards. Three white men with gray ponytails, all wearing brown coveralls, were waiting for their tool chests to be unloaded from the cart. I recognized the island dialect one Filipino family was speaking, but most of the other voices were in languages I didn't recognize at all. A thin Ethiopian was standing next to a massive Tongan who was shouldering his way through a group of men in sleeveless shirts speaking Spanish.

A tall white man with a round face, a knit cabby's hat, and a well-trimmed beard elbowed through them toward me and thrust out his hand.

"You're Cecil Younger. Well, how the heck are ya?" he said in a booming voice.

I shook his hand reflexively and nodded blankly, for I wasn't feeling perky enough to be met by a cop.

He kept pumping my hand. "I'm Glen. I'm the Chief of Police."

My grip loosened and I tried to withdraw my hand but the chief held tight and eased me into a quieter corner across from the car rental kiosk. He leaned down until his face was very close to mine.

"You know, Cecil, I have a friend in Anchorage who used to be on the force here. She didn't like the weather much and she got sick of not being able to eat out as much as she liked . . . you know how it is? Well, anyway, she got a job as airport security in Anchorage. She gives me a call from time to time, just to let me know what's coming."

I finally pulled my hand away and took a step back. "If this is about that guy peeing in his airsickness bag, I didn't see a thing." I started to walk away, but the chief took me by the elbow and I jerked away from him.

"Am I under arrest? Are you detaining me for any reason other than to welcome me to your fair city?"

The chief let go. Smiling broadly so that his face took on the jolly look of a jack-o'-lantern, he spread his arms. "Hey, relax, man. I'm honestly here to welcome you to Dutch." He took off his cap and in an overdrawn gesture wiped his brow with it.

"Whoa! Don't be so touchy. Why are you so touchy? You act like you get run out of towns a lot. What? You get run out of towns a lot or what?" His voice had the twang of a New York cabdriver. As he stepped back, his blue raincoat hung open and I could see his badge clipped to his belt next to a .45 automatic.

"Well, thank you for the welcome," I said and walked to where the handlers were unloading luggage from the cart onto a stainless steel bin.

The chief persisted. "Listen, I'm serious. Cecil, let me take you where you're going. If I can help you with anything while you're here I'd be happy to."

The toolboxes slammed down hard against the side of the baggage area and the three ponytailed men in coveralls lugged them away, leaning into them as they limped out to the open truck that was waiting beyond the double doors. I saw my pack and as I reached for it, the chief grabbed it up. He spun and looked at me. He started speaking before I had a chance to open my mouth. His voice was calm but strong with the tone of some authentic authority.

"Let me drive you, Cecil. We need to talk." He strode toward the doors past the towering Tongan, who smiled as the chief went by but did not unfold his arms. I stood where I was. The chief turned.

"Come on. Come on," he said, stamping his feet and laughing as if he were calling a puppy. "Come on. Look! I'm stealing your bag. You can have me arrested. I can pistol-whip myself in my own jail. Come on, Cecil . . ."

The Tongan was smiling broadly and shaking his head as I walked past.

The chief drove a new four-wheel-drive Ford. He opened the front passenger door and then went around to the driver's side. He threw my bag in the backseat. As he climbed in, he keyed the radio mike on the dash and told his dispatcher he was inbound and would be out of service for a few minutes. Then he turned down the volume and started the engine.

"You're from Sitka, right?"

I shook my head.

"Sitka is a great town. You know, it's so pretty there. You get a—what?—hundred inches of rain a year? That's not all that bad. I don't know what we get here. It's blowing so hard I don't know if it's really raining here or not. You know they say it rains in Siberia and falls in the Aleutians."

I didn't reply. The road from the airport was a washboard of hard gravel ruts. The beachfront was a tangle of cement chunks, rebar, and washed-up cable and ropes from commercial gear.

"Sitka's a pretty peaceful little town, isn't it, Cecil?"

"I believe so. Yes." I was wondering if I needed to invoke my right to an attorney. After all, I couldn't very well jump out of a moving police car.

"That's what I always thought, too." The chief was staring at me as he drove and I was getting a little nervous because we were drifting into the center of the road and a tractor trailer was becoming large in front of us. The chief glanced back at the road, honked, and then swerved back into his lane.

"Yes, sir, that's what I always thought. Peaceful town. That's why I was kind of surprised when a guy from Sitka just flies in here yesterday and tries to kill one of our local citizens."

"Really?" I said, trying not to sound too Sam Spade-ish or anything.

"That's right. Have him up in my concrete hotel right now. Apparently his daughter was killed and for some reason he is angry with a man called Simon Delaney. I don't really know why. Do you have any reason to know why?"

"*Didn't* kill him?" I asked, ducking his question to me.

"No . . . no. Didn't kill him." The chief waved to a cabdriver in a van painted with bright polka dots. Then he said to me with a lively tone in his voice, "Don't ride with that guy, Cecil," indicating the cab that just passed. "He charges more than everybody else . . . unless you want to buy some drugs from him. But you wouldn't want to be buying cocaine from him, would you?" The chief laughed, a high, nasal whinny. Then he went on without waiting for my answer to the drug-purchasing question.

"No. Didn't kill him. There was a fracas down at the recreation hall. Not all that unusual, I guess. This guy was yelling at Mr. Delaney. You know Mr. Delaney, right?"

He turned to me, waiting for something, even if it was a nod of agreement. I looked out the window to the Bering Sea.

"So anyway . . . this Mexican-looking guy is just standing there holding a pretty big folding knife when my officers come and he's screaming something in Spanish. One of my officers speaks a little, you know. Probably high school stuff or maybe a little vacation Spanish, but anyway he says this Mexican guy is screaming that the dead are always with us, that they can't be forgotten, and how would Mr. Delaney like to find out for himself. Something like that."

"Did Delaney get hurt?" I asked.

"Hurt? Well . . . pushed and threatened with a knife. I suppose I could hold Mr. Ramirez for a felony assault. Mr. David Ramirez. You know *him*, right?" The chief used a tone of voice indicating I would be a complete dummy if I didn't admit to knowing David Ramirez.

The chief continued talking and looking straight at me as he drove. "I mean, the knife is bad. Mr. Delaney could reasonably be afraid of serious physical injury, but that all depends, really, if he thought the old man really wanted to hurt him. What do you think, Cecil?"

We stopped at some road construction. There were

several pickup trucks ahead of us. The one directly in front had a gigantic Irish wolfhound riding in the back.

"Ask Simon Delaney," I offered.

"Well, I did, and that's a good point. It really is. After all, he is the victim in this case. But Mr. Delaney doesn't really want to speak to me. I don't know why. Do you have any thoughts on this?"

I shook my head with as much ambiguity as I could manage.

"No, I didn't think you would." The chief looked down carefully at his steering wheel. "Oh. Hey!" he said in mock surprise. "You aren't here to interview Simon Delaney, are you?"

I looked at the chief and did not interrupt his routine. I was beginning to wonder if he practiced in front of the mirror at home. "I would like to talk with Delaney myself. Maybe I could help you find him. But all that depends . . ." the chief said, and he smiled an evil kind of grin that made me regret coming out to the Aleutians in the first place.

The traffic started to move and we crossed a broad wooden bridge and drove up a muddy street to the sprawling metal building that I assumed was the police station. The chief pulled around back of the building and parked his car.

"You see my point?" He leveled his stare at me and there was no comedy in his voice anymore.

"No, I'm not sure I do," I told him.

"My point is this: I've talked to the Sitka Police, Cecil. They think you're involved in a murder case in their jurisdiction. They need an interview with Simon Delaney about their case, but he is apparently not talking to anyone. So if you are going to talk to him, I'm going to be there with you."

"I suppose that will be up to Mr. Delaney," I offered and shrugged my shoulders like a sulky adolescent, which I think irritated the chief.

He grabbed my elbow as if he were going to lead me to detention. "Let me tell you something, friend." His voice was taut and his skin was turning ruddy. "You are going to play this game by my rules or I'll find something to charge you with. Believe me, you might end up being grateful if I did do that. My jail may be the safest place for you." He let go of my elbow and leaned back against the car seat. Then he calmed noticeably, remembering, I suppose, that he had me to himself, in his car, on his island in the Bering Sea.

"Takes a long time to get a lawyer here," he said as he set the parking brake. "I'm not threatening you, you understand, Cecil, and I'm not trying to make you feel . . . unwelcome or anything. I'm just warning you of a problem I see on the horizon."

He stared me straight in the eyes until I nodded in agreement.

"This town has a reputation for violence," the chief told me. "It's not all undeserved, but see, we don't really get that many killings here. Disappearances . . . sure, and funnylooking suicides that get written up that way, but mostly we have a lot of beatings and knifings, kind of recreational violence. We don't get many bloody vendettas here in this town. Well, we didn't until Marcus and your Mr. Delaney came and set up shop." He handed me my bag from the backseat. "No, most of our bloody vendettas are over the school board or the city engineers tearing up the streets." He slapped me on the shoulder and got out of the car.

"You might find Simon Delaney in town. Just go on down the hill and head for the church and look around. It's an old red barn-looking place. Simon's, not the church. Used to be the roller rink. Simon's place, that is . . ." The chief scratched his head, pretending to be fuddled. "I'll see you around probably," he shouted at me in his hearty voice.

The chief punched the combination on the back door, opened it, and disappeared into the station.

I started off down the hill. The wind had freshened to maybe twenty knots, and the waves were pushing up on the steep cobbled beach that carved a crescent into the island. Out to sea I could see the black curtain of a squall moving across the water. I walked past Dutch Harbor's post office and the community building, across a stream running from a lake through the valley and down to the sea.

A broad dirt avenue paralleled the beach. To my right up the hill was a cemetery dotted with Russian crosses. To my left was the Russian church with its weathered white paint and onion dome. Sitting squarely on the cross atop the onion dome was an immature eagle, his brown and white feathers ruffled by the wind. Down on the beach, tangles of line were knotted around pieces of broken shipping pallets, and I saw a mature eagle walking clumsily along the stones, pecking at a snarl of netting. Then I noticed three more eagles on the bank watching the first. Only then did it occur to me that without any trees the eagles sit on the ground.

I went to the left and walked down the avenue toward the church, past kids on rickety bikes blustering down the short side streets as if they were pieces of paper blown by the wind. A German shepherd was tied to a clothesline and a native woman with what I'm sure was a parrot on her shoulder was walking between two of the blue wooden frame houses. The parrot's long tail feathers fluttered in a gust of wind; the woman touched the bird with the same hand she had her cigarette in.

I passed a couple of little shops and turned and saw a black sign with a painting of a humpback whale and white lettering. The sign had the name of a bar that I recognized from somewhere but I couldn't quite place where. I was pondering this when the door to the bar banged open behind me and a blond woman in jeans and a tank top pushed a man out onto the dirt street. She was jabbing him with her index finger and shrieking at the top of her lungs.

"I don't have to listen to this shit! I was raised better than that! You want to talk that kind of shit, take it home to your old lady!"

The man fell flat onto his butt and sat there looking stunned as if he had fallen out of the sky. He was a white man with a long mustache, wearing a thin padded jacket ripped along the length of the right arm so that the synthetic insulation spilled out past the seams where someone had tried to tape it together with hundred-mile-an-hour tape. The man had his pipe fitter's ball cap on cockeyed. He started to smile, but when he turned and saw me watching him his face turned sour.

"What the *fuck* you looking at?" he slurred.

"I was thinking about going in the bar but it looks a little risky," I offered in a soft voice.

He groaned and gestured wildly in the general direction of the blond woman and the rest of North America.

"What am I going to do? I just got to *talk* to the bitch," he drawled out. He tried to get his feet up underneath himself but failed. Then he rolled over onto his hands and knees and worked the problem of his wandering center of gravity from there. He beckoned with his hands, clawlike, toward her.

"Come here now. Come on, baby, help me back up. I'm just trying to tell you how I FEEL! It's not like I'm asking you to give me head or nothing." His voice had that nasal kind of tremor that I remembered from my own years of such entreaties.

The wind was hitting harder now and rain was starting to spatter down like nails onto the dirt. A gust carried a strand of the woman's blond hair above her head, revealing mouse brown roots underneath. She snapped at her lighter and pinched a cigarette tightly between her lips. The wind battered her back against the wooden siding.

"Come on, baby!" the man on his knees wheezed,

barely audible above the squall. "I'm just trying to tell you how I FEEL!"

The woman dropped the unlit cigarette and her lighter back into the leather case she had been carrying in her left hand. She looked at the man for a moment, then took one unsteady step backward toward the door and kicked him full in the face with the force of a placekicker. He rolled onto his back and lay for a second, but as she opened the door, his outstretched hand grabbed her ankle, pulling her back.

The eagle on the church flew back behind the church and up the narrow streambed. The squall seemed to blacken out the sun as it buffeted the houses. I heard the woman scream and as I walked toward them, the white man, who now had a broken nose pushed to the side of his face, was sitting astride the blond woman's chest, pounding her face with his fists.

I was three feet from them when the door to the bar opened wide and men started pouring out. Men with dark skin and straight black hair came rumbling out of the bar. They were wearing T-shirts with the names of different beers on the front, and they tried to pull the white man off the woman. Then three white men came out. Apparently thinking their buddy had been jumped by the darker-skinned men, they started screaming and pushing. I stopped advancing.

Even though the rain was starting to fall more evenly, now the wind was strong enough to curl up dust. There were men rolling in the dirt, clawing and pummeling each other. Someone's shirt was ripped. Blood smeared on white fabric. The blond woman screamed. Curses in English and Spanish popped like lightning. Somewhere above the wind and the grunting I heard the thin ribbon of a siren. It looked like six pairs of men were squared off and fighting now. A dozen patrons were standing along the wall. They all held drinks in their hands. A woman in an apron was talking into a cellular phone. The blond woman was sobbing and pressing a bar rag to her face. The first white man lay unconscious near her legs. Occasionally, crying, the blond woman would reach out with the heel of her cowboy boot and kick him in the head. Someone gave her a shot glass full of whiskey.

Two police trucks pulled up. The chief stepped out of the first one and waved to the woman with the cell phone. The other three officers walked slowly to the fight and stood like observers. The chief smiled at me.

"What I tell you, Cecil?"

I nodded. "It doesn't look like anybody's got their knives out yet," I told him.

As he walked toward the patrons of the bar, the chief started calling out names and waving, speaking in a soothing voice.

"Fernando. Carlo. Bobbie. Fellas! Fellas! Why are we fighting?" The chief stood with his arms spread wide. People started to retreat as if their rock had just been turned over. The other police officers stood with their hands on their belts. The crowd of onlookers started to disperse. Two of the dark-haired fighters who were on top stopped slugging and immediately walked back into the bar. One took off around the corner. The heroes on the bottom started screaming and threatening, and as they did the officers walked over and stepped on their chests.

Only two serious combatants were left: two young white men with long black hair who were lying in the street, which was quickly becoming mud. One of the men had blood across his face and neck. His teeth were clamped down hard on the ear of the other. Snot and blood smeared down his upper lip, disappearing into his clenched teeth. Both of the men were growling, their breath heaving out, although the one who was having his ear chewed had a screeching whine mixed with his grunting.

It's rare for a bar fight to last much over fifteen

seconds. Most of the fighters can't maintain the aerobic flow much past that.

The chief squatted down and spoke softly to the two men. "Okay, boys, I tell you what. If you get up now and stay quiet for the rest of the night we'll call it good. But if you keep this up I'm going to throw both your asses in jail."

The top man sprang up onto his feet. Two officers took him by the arms. The other fighter rolled up on his seat, his earlobe flapping down from a strand of skin, sticky blood spitting down as his ear hung against his neck. The chief helped him up and led him over to the aid car that was just rolling down the street.

The chief walked over to the blond woman who was still sitting against the building. He knelt down next to her and her eyes watched him warily.

"Christine, you want to go to the clinic?"

The woman looked at the chief and drank the last of the whiskey from the glass. She took the bloody bar rag away from her face.

"I want this son of a bitch to go to jail." She kicked the unconscious white man once more. The chief didn't flinch.

"Well, we'll take him in, Christine. But we need to patch him up and then take some statements. I don't know yet if we can charge him."

Christine's eyes smoldered. "That's okay," she whispered, her voice shaky. Then in one quick motion she smashed the heavy shot glass on the steps. Her hand became a carnation of bright blood. The chief reached for her but she leaned forward and thrust the jagged end of the glass into the throat of the white man at her feet.

"Oh, Christ, Christine," the chief muttered, as a garden hose spray of arterial blood shot wildly into the rain and wind. Two officers grabbed her by the shoulders and dragged her toward their truck. The fallen man's blood spurted with each heartbeat. "Oh dear, oh dear, oh dear," the chief kept murmuring. The aid car had pulled away with the other in-jured fighter and now the spray of blood from the stabbed man pulsed more slowly onto the chief's pants.

"Well, there's nothing else for it," he said wearily, and he jabbed his index finger into the throat of the white man. He twisted his hand around, feeling for the cut artery, and then he held it still. The spurting stopped. The white man gurgled and tried to roll away.

"Cecil, can you give me a hand here." The chief spoke to me as if he were asking for the salt. I came forward and knelt next to him.

"Help me get him on his side. I got my hands full here but we have to make sure he can breathe." The woman with the cellular phone was pounding on her handset and the officers were talking to the aid car that was now making a U-turn with the other bleeder.

The blond woman screamed from the open window of the police truck: "Chief! Hey, Chief!"

"What is it, Christine?" The chief spoke evenly.

The light bar on the roof of the truck was flashing. The wet buildings pulsed blue in the rain. One officer was rolling up the window as Christine stuck her head out to stop him.

"Chief! Have you ever been in love?" Rain and tears tracked mascara down her cheeks.

The chief stared at her for a long moment, not say-ing a thing. Then he shook his head. "Yeah," he said. "Yeah, I have," and he smiled as the truck pulled away with Christine and rounded the corner into the dark.

He looked back up at me, one hand stuck down into the bleeder's throat and the other propping him up. The chief patted the bleeding white man as the other officers helped the aid car back around to the front door of the bar.

"Hey, Cecil. What the heck are you doing here anyway?" the chief asked suddenly.

"What do you mean?" I asked, a little distracted by the groaning of the white man on the ground.

"Well, you missed Simon Delaney's place. It's back that way." He gestured with his blood-spattered chin. "It's a block back from the beach, just a little way down the street. You must have walked the beach, huh?"

I nodded, and then the other personnel moved in and I got out of the way. The chief and the injured man disappeared into a crowd of uniforms. A woman in a bomber jacket was fixing an IV. A man in a fireman's coat was pulling out gauze pads by the handful. I waved, rinsed some blood spatter off my hand in a puddle, then walked away.

The street was almost dark but I could make out the dark barnlike structure on the left side of the dirt road. The windows were boarded up and one of the sheets of plywood clattered against the frame as the wind battered it. Across the street was a restaurant that advertised pizza and Mexican food. One floodlight was mounted on the wall, shining up on the front of the old roller rink.

WILD BILL'S ROUND BALL ROUNDUP
WORKERS' COMMUNITY CENTER AND
MUTUAL AID SOCIETY
also
THE AMERICAN SOBRIETY ASSOCIATION
All workers and their families welcome

There was a narrow front door. The flooring was soft underneath. Just inside was a bench and counter where the skate rental kiosk had once been. Above the door that led to the old rink was a large hand-lettered sign on green board with white lettering:

WELCOME WORKERS
YOU ARE A WORKER IF YOU:
Gut fish, change diapers, fill out schedules,

pull gear, drive skiffs, do dishes, baby-sit, weld metal, drive trucks, answer phones, program computers, sign checks, or volunteer your efforts without pay. In short, if you strive for any piece of the larger good, you are a worker.

All workers deserve some of the "good life." We don't all have to be rich but we deserve to live without fear in a free and peaceable society.

THE RULES OF THE HALL

All racism, prejudice, and class hatred must be left outside / No bullies or perverts / Respect for women, children, and all peaceable patrons will be enforced at all times / All knives stay in their sheaths / No guns of any kind / Don't bust stuff up / If you can't resolve your differences peacefully the other patrons will resolve them for you.

Remember: Together we create all wealth.
Divided, we create a mess that somebody's got
to clean up.

I could hear the sound of a basketball banging on the wooden floor inside. Suddenly, in the door frame of the inner door stood a very large man with a broad mocha-colored face and tremendous forearms. He was grinning broadly and had a small diamond in his right ear. He wore an enormous red T-shirt with white letters reading ONE BIG WORLD

"I bet you're a private dick from Sitka. I'm Marcus. I talked to you yesterday when you did that fake package bit. I'm sorry you missed Simon. He's not around."

Chapter Five

Inside, the room was lit with fluorescent fixtures above a warped maple wood floor. The hall was unusually decrepit and eerie. In the corner, a man who looked to be from southeast Asia was bouncing a basketball under a bent hoop without netting. All around the edges of the room were maybe a dozen pinball machines. The inside of the old roller rink was throbbing with flashing lights, the cacophony of ringing bells, and the clack of pinball flippers. A few men and women were standing around the machines drinking soda and coffee. In the rafters was a double section of plywood with a painting of a large white man in an old-fashioned suit. He wore a big grin under his stiff straw boater hat. A painted banner under his portrait read BIG BILL HAYWOOD . . . GONE BUT NOT FORGOTTEN.

I turned and looked over the door where there was another badly drawn portrait of a bearded man with wire-rimmed glasses. The banner read PETER KROPOTKIN—ANARCHY AND MUTUAL AID. Then I noticed that above every pinball machine there were smaller portraits. Men with pointed beards and wire-rimmed glasses. Women in white blouses standing on speaker's platforms exhorting crowds. Each scene had a short quotation under it. Off to the left was an alcove with four broken-down couches and some chairs. Groups of men and women were sitting and talking. There was a cart stacked with juice and soda. There were racks with pamphlets and government forms featuring everything from change-of-address and voter registration to blank Freedom of Information requests and pamphlets entitled "Immigration and Naturalization Service: Know Your Rights."

"Simon said you were working for the old man?" Marcus was walking away from me toward an overstuffed couch near the darkest corner of the hall.

"How did Simon know that?" I asked.

Marcus shrugged his shoulders. "Don't know. But Simon said you were going to try and get the old man off on some insanity thing."

"What else did Simon tell you?"

Again Marcus shrugged his shoulders. He settled down into the old couch.

I looked around the hall. Bells rang and lights from the machines spilled out like tropical drinks across the floor. Men and women standing in sneakers or rubber boots thumped against the machines and worked the flippers. I could smell popcorn, dust, layers of mildew, sweat, and heating oil. Over the years, these old odors must have soaked into the wooden building like the rain.

Marcus slapped me on the back. "I know what you're thinking," he said theatrically and grabbed a couple of boxes of juice off the cart. Then he motioned me to sit on one of the leaking overstuffed couches. I sank deeply into the springs.

"You're thinking, 'What kind of ideological bullshit is this?' Aren't you?"

I shook my head, but Marcus went right on. There was a basketball at his feet. He lifted it up and spun it on his index finger. My eye caught the cold glitter of his earring.

"Don't worry, man. This isn't an ideology. It's a force of nature." He smiled broadly. "There is nothing—no program, no computer game—that can match the unpredictability of a round ball interacting in a complex environment. Arcade managers found this out when the secondhand buyers were still making a killing selling off the old pinball machines."

"But video games are still more popular."

"They're not games anymore. Only nominally."

"What are they?"

"Video games are environments. Or rather they are locations in the larger electronic environment the corporate world is transforming world culture into. You don't play electronic games. They play *you*. You can't cheat at electronic games but you can still cheat at pinball. That's part of its charm."

I looked around at the fishery workers playing pinball and talking. "So, pinball is in the vanguard of world revolution?"

Marcus continued smiling and put the ball in his lap. "I am not a revolutionary. Most of the people who come in here think all this stuff about empowerment and self-expression is a joke. I don't really care so much what they think. I just want them to *do* something. I'm a social director." He held his hands wide as if he were leading me to the buffet. "This is a social club for working people. A place they can get together to talk and play. I encourage them to express themselves. To vote. To tell their bosses what they want. Some do . . . most don't, and that's okay with me. I'm not an ideologue. People say that anarchy is dead, but they're mistaken. It's like saying that weather is dead." He bounced the ball next to his knees.

"I'm not following you," I said and sucked on my juice.

Marcus leaned back and stared up at the ceiling of

darkened trusses and rafters. "Anarchy is the leaderless expression of the whole. Anarchy operates in gossip, games, weather. Gossip survives everywhere and it isn't the expression of the elite. Gossip's so successful that the consumer-based electronic media tries imitating it. Weather patterns are formed by combined forces of the earth expressing themselves in the atmosphere. The resultant compromise causes weather patterns that fall into parameters but are not predictable and are certainly not hierarchical."

A young woman with jet black hair falling across her forehead walked by. She rolled her eyes as she heard Marcus's tone of voice, indicating to me that she had heard this sermon before.

"The people express themselves communally. It is a force of nature. It escapes rhetoric just as the weather escapes the weatherman," Marcus said with a self-satisfied grin, and he sat back to let that sit, then added, "Anarchy is natural. What is unnatural is the stifling of people's desires." Before I could respond to that, he leaned forward again. "The old people knew that. You've read about Raven, Hermes, Ananzi, Coyote: anarchists and the creators of the universe."

"Is David Ramirez a trickster?" I asked without fanfare.

Marcus did not change his expression. His eyes still glittered beneath his hooded lids. He started spinning the basketball on the tip of his finger again. He ignored my question and went on with his sermon. "Now of course there is a very long and distinguished tradition of anarchist thought that evolved right along with the industrial society. Mikhail Bakunin, Peter Kropotkin, up through Karl Marx and even today, there are thinkers who maintain that capitalism is rotten to the core. The first priority of capitalist government is that profits must grow. There will be no social progress unless capitalism changes this basic premise:

No stable currency, no civil rights, no feminism, no environmentalism until the corporate and class structure serves all the people equally, rather than garnering private wealth for a few."

"Is that what you think?" I asked, a little numbed.

Marcus leaned his massive forearms on his knees. "The culture of America is soaked in capitalism. If it were honestly rotten to the core then we would not be able to be outraged by its injustices. But—" and he slapped his hands together. "It's not for me to decide. I just want to hear from the workers. I will listen to them. They will gossip, they will tell stories. They will express themselves as long as they are encouraged to do so."

"And what if all the workers want is to be rich capitalists?" I shot out.

Marcus's eyes darkened. "Of course they want to be rich. You'd have to be a fool not to want to be rich in this culture but eventually the workers, through collective understanding, will discover this promise is a lie. That it is not possible for all of them to be rich." He picked up the basketball. "That is when the splinter groups and revolutionaries move toward the stage." He bounced the ball. "It will be messy." He squinted at me. "Poor people are not always going to be content just killing each other."

I was getting irritated with his reasoning. "Yeah, well, my problems are important, too, you know. And right now my problem is finding your leader. Where is Simon Delaney?"

Marcus reached over and slapped me on the back, hard. His hand felt as large as my collarbone. The young woman with the jet black hair was laughing and saying, "I gotta go, man. I'll see you tomorrow. You'll be in, right?"

"Yeah. Thanks, Lisa. I'll be around." Marcus waved and the young woman walked toward the door and out past a girl who was fishing for coins in her pocket.

"Simon isn't my leader." Marcus's voice became a shade darker. It made me sit up straighter. Pay closer attention. He went on, "Simon is going through a period where he is acting against his own interest. Acting against *our* own interests. I've got to bring him back. He's got to collect himself . . . before it ends badly for him."

Marcus fell silent. We sat still in the clatter of the flashing machines. Finally he spoke up.

"Simon will help that old man out of his problems. Hell, that old man was a Wobbly, an anarcho-syndicalist." Marcus smiled as he rolled the big, strange-sounding word around in his mouth. "Wobblies believed in uniting all of the workers into one big union. They predicted that trade unionism would end up serving the masters, and they were right."

Again he was smiling broadly. The large plates of his palms, creased and buttery-white, were holding up the world.

"We're a long way from one big union." He looked at his hands as he searched for words. "All I want—all Simon wants is for working people not to feel dead." He paused.

"America hates the people who do the shit work," he said. "If they aren't rich they must deserve what they get."

"Did Angela Ramirez deserve what she got?" I asked him.

His eyes were torches now. His voice was low and unsteady, unsmiling. "I know Angela . . . *knew* . . . Angela. It doesn't surprise me . . . the way she died. Thousands of people a year are killed by poverty."

"I thought Simon killed her?"

"You're fishing, aren't you? The chief said you were a clown but I think he misjudged you. Simon didn't kill Angela. Simon said the old man killed her."

Marcus got up and grabbed us both another box of juice. This time he sat down next to me.

"The chief told me your name was Younger. Cecil. Is that it?" He held out his hand and took mine in a friendly grip. His hand was smooth but I could feel the scar running across its palm.

A van pulled up outside the window and people started walking in through the back door. Three dark-skinned men in work shirts, casual slacks, and plastic boots, with books under their arms. A couple of young white women with dark hair. Both had scarves across their foreheads and they were wearing running clothes and broken-over sneakers. Two young men with shiny black skin. All moved to the corner of the room. Each of them smiled at Marcus and one of the young women pulled a podium to the center of the room. The rest pulled chairs from around us, and Marcus and I walked away from the group so they could begin their meeting. Many of the players on the machines stopped playing and walked over to listen. The young woman stood at the podium and in a clear voice that had the lilt of an eastern European accent began:

"Hi. I'm Sylvia. This is our meeting of the American Sobriety Association. As I see so many new faces in the crowd, I think I'll start off."

Marcus walked around and asked the last two players on the tables to stop their game. He handed them some juice, motioning them to come over to the meeting. Out of the corner of my eye I saw a large man with a mustache walk past the window.

"Well, as I said, I'm Sylvia. I'm a mother and a worker. I'm sliming fish this season and I work on the freezer side during swing shifts over at Talbot's. I'm good at what I do. My kids are with their father while I'm up here working. My kids are good kids, good citizens. I'm proud of them. I'm proud of my work record. But sometimes I act against my own interests. I sometimes drink too much and I sometimes take cocaine . . ."

I saw David Ramirez walk into the hall. Angela's father had a gaff hook in his right hand. The gaff was two-thirds the length of a baseball bat and it had a metal spike curving wickedly from the thick end. The handle was narrow and taped like a ball bat. He must have taken it from one of the skiffs that was hauled out on the river bank. He came toward the sobriety gathering, lowering the gaff down past his waist. I tapped Marcus on the shoulder and then walked toward the door.

Sylvia continued, "Today I believe that sobriety is a revolutionary act. Being *in* this world and clearly expressing yourself is the first step in revolutionary change of any kind. When I say 'revolution,' I'm talking about the dramatic reversal of the status . . ."

Marcus turned and saw David Ramirez raise the gaff hook above his head. Marcus ducked and rolled across the floor. The meeting around the broken couches swiftly scattered. Sylvia calmly walked toward the door, where two of the older men had tripped on their way out. The two older men were scrambling to get up when Sylvia stepped on their backs to exit the building. Screams and words I didn't understand scattered out into the rain. Most of the men had jumped back toward the shadows near the corners of the hall. But Marcus stood to face David Ramirez, who was shaking the tip of the gaff hook in his face.

"Where has he gone?" David Ramirez asked in a smoldering voice.

"Go home, Mr. Ramirez." Marcus said it evenly, without raising his voice and without a trace of fear.

Ramirez swung at the empty air, then again into the guts of the old couch. Marcus pushed between the two men who were helping each other up in the doorway. He walked calmly out the door and Ramirez slapped again at the cushioning of the old couch with the gaff hook. He pulled out a spring; it flopped out like a sprung clockworks.

David Ramirez stared at me. He gestured with the gaff hook. "I found out from the police in Sitka he had come here. You warned Simon Delaney I was coming. Don't do it again." His voice was surprisingly businesslike.

I nodded my head in a circle, trying both to agree and disagree as quickly as I could while walking backward out the door. Down the muddy street I could see Marcus's broad back slicked down by the rain as he strode past the lights of the houses facing the street, toward the bridge. I could hear the sucking sound as his shoes pounded down into the mud. I headed after him.

Across the bridge I looked around. The rain washed down on me so hard I couldn't feel the drops. I had my pack slung over my shoulders. It was slimy with water and slid around the material of my coat. The wind gusted so hard that the rain blasted me sideways. Two hundred yards up the treeless hill I could see the figure of a person switchbacking the steep terrain toward a little cut in the ridge. The figure stopped occasionally and looked down toward the valley where I was. Behind me, David Ramirez stood in the middle of the street and I could see the lights of a police car coming down the hill from the station. Ramirez flung the gaff hook in the ditch, and after looking up and down the street he walked quickly away from me toward the music of the jukebox in the bar. There was a good crowd there and he would slide in and be relatively invisible when and if the cops poked their heads inside.

Pelted by rain, I headed up the hill, following the faint trace of a little-used path in the grass. The trail was deceptively steep. The grass was slick and the rain buffeted me so that I had to lean into the hill and steady myself with my hands as I made it up to the notch in the hill. Just behind the notch was a weathered gray shack. There was the flicker of candlelight inside.

The porch flooring was rotten under my feet. Rusty

nails pulled against the bleached wood. Metal roofing rattled as the wind pushed up underneath it.

"That you, Cecil?" I followed Marcus's voice inside the door. Marcus was sitting on a sleeping bag on the floor. He was toweling himself off with his shirt.

"Hey. You really are a detective, man. You found me. Is Papa Ramirez coming up the hill?"

"No," I said as I stepped across his legs and made my way to the other side of the lit plumber's candle he had set on an upturned milk crate. "He took off the other way. The police were coming."

"Good." Marcus dug under his sleeping bag and pulled out a dry sweatshirt and pulled it on. He threw me the wet shirt, gesturing that it was okay to dry myself off with it.

"The Japs bombed Dutch Harbor during the war. Just once, but it scared the army bad. They had everybody in big central barracks and after the bombing they moved them out into these cabanas in the hills. There are dozens of them left. They belong to the Native Corporation now and they are hard on squatters, but you can still find one like this to keep a few emergency supplies in. It's my cave behind the waterfall." He smiled at me, arching his eyebrows.

He reached again under his sleeping bag and pulled out a plastic bag with some dried fish and candy bars zipped inside. He took out a strip of fish and handed it to me. "So, did the old man give you a bunch of money to help him beat the murder charge?" He squinted over the guttering wax candle.

I bit into the fish. It tasted rich with oil and the flavor of the woods. Marcus took a bite of his fish and gestured wildly around the bubble of light in the shack.

"You know, they had some fifty thousand troops stationed here during the war. I don't know if it's true or not, but people say the army was concerned because after being out on this rock the men were getting drunk and having sex with one another. Isn't that something?" He took another bite of the fish and chewed as he spoke. "What do you think? You think all those men were homosexual?"

I kept drying myself off and hoped by not answering I could stay out of this conversation.

"Shit, no!" he blurted. "What, all fifty thousand of them were gay and after VJ day they moved in with their lovers? Hell, no. Well, maybe some of them did and, God bless them, I hope they're happy."

He threw me a candy bar. It landed on my lap and I undid the wrapper. I was chewing as he went on.

"No. Those men were just doing what they were supposed to be doing. Those men were just filling any hole they could find. The urge for life is relentless. Nature fills every niche and most of them are dead ends." He was laughing and chewing. I could see the pink flesh of the dried salmon swirling around his tongue and teeth. "I mean, only a relentless and leaderless system of life would fill everything possible with potential, just on the off chance that one day one of these seeds might take root. It's like the spawning of the coral at the Great Barrier Reef, except instead of one night of the year it happens all the time."

I moved away from the candle and stood up nervously to dry the back of my neck. "Does this story have a moral?" I asked. "Or is it another revolutionary parable?"

"No." Marcus found a tin cup by the candle and held it out the window to catch some rain. "What did the old man tell you about Simon?"

"He said Simon knew where Ole Hanson was."

"Ole Hanson? Really. Man, that's some old stuff there." Marcus kept eating and chuckling to himself. "Speaking of parables. Did he tell you the one about the cormorant and the Japanese fisherman?"

"Yeah, he did."

Marcus pulled the cup back in and it was overflowing with water. He quickly sipped off the rim to keep the water from spilling. Then he sat back down next to me.

"I met Simon Delaney six years ago. Down on the Homer spit. I was some happy little slave working on the slime line. I had studied history at the University of Washington, played some football, and you know I was one of those *good* colored people. I was going to make enough money to buy a house of my own and raise a family of good colored children. Simon used that Japanese fisherman story on me."

Marcus's eyes glittered up at me in the flutter of the light from the candle. "You know, that old man was a hell of a radical in his day. He bummed around all over the West: grain harvest, logging camps, fruit pickers, anything. He could put up a free-speech fight in any town, under any conditions."

"He didn't seem to care much for Centralia, Washington, though."

"You ever been there?" He offered me some rainwater and I took it.

"No." I handed the cup back to him.

"It's a tough little town, in love with antiques. I've been there with Simon. His grandma's bar is still there. It's broken down, but beautiful. Simon stays there at the bar whenever he goes back to visit."

We listened to the rain shudder down on the torn metal roofing.

"The old man tell you about the massacre?" Marcus asked.

"No."

"Oh, man, you say you working for the old man and you don't know about the massacre? You're just a baby in this thing. We've got to take care of that."

A gust blasted the shack and the candle flickered.

"Tomorrow I'll tell you about the massacre and

you'll be so happy to hear about it you're going to give me all that money that's in your backpack."

I started to move protectively toward my gear. Marcus waved his hand in front of his face and started to laugh.

"I was fishing, Cecil. I was just fishing. I didn't know you had the money. But by the way you put a grip on that pack . . . I guess you do."

Another gust rattled the sides of the shack. This time the candle sputtered and went out.

"Yeah, I know you've got the money. And tomorrow you're going to give it to me," the large man said, and his voice filled the room like the wind.

Chapter Six

By morning, the wind had died. I was wet and stiff, with my head resting on the pack that still held the money I took from William Flynn's cabin. Sun vented in through the cracks in the walls, tracking like icicles in the room. Marcus was gone. I bolted out the door, stumbling on the loose boards and bumping into him stretching in the icy wind.

"Man, oh, man, quite a day so far." He stretched again, his curly black hair crushed to one side of his head, his eyes pinched shut.

By daylight, I saw that the shack sat in a tiny bowl on the grassy ridge. The wet grass was tan with only a hint of green, like a fine dust over the hill. I couldn't see the ocean but I could smell it on the wind. An eagle circled and a bunting hopped in the tall grass near the shallow stream tipping over the edge of the bowl. Overhead, islands of white clouds tumbled and pulled apart in the sky.

Marcus opened his eyes. "I don't think Angela's daddy really intends to kill me. Let's go to town and you can buy me brunch at the new hotel."

We walked the ridge line, staying above the town of Unalaska and off the road system, until we came upon a massive concrete bunker topped with what looked like a twenty-foot-tall bald eagle. I stopped and almost stumbled down the slope. When the scene snapped into focus I could see that the bunker, although massively built, was constructed very low to the ground. The stunted trees gave it the illusion of being much farther away than it really was. Marcus laughed at the expression on my face and headed toward the bridge that connected Unalaska to the port of Dutch Harbor.

We crossed behind the police station and down to the bridge. A rain squall moved through and I lost my footing on the last pitch down to the road. I rolled twenty feet through the mud, so my face was smeared and my pants were slick with a reddish-brown paste by the time we stood in the hotel lobby waiting to be seated for brunch.

Sunlight sent rainbow slices across the carpets. The carpets here were soft and deep and I could hear my shoes squishing across them as we made our way to our table. All the fixtures were polished glass. There was a line at the buffet where steam tables were set up with silver dishes: bacon and king crab, smoked salmon quiche lorraine, biscuits and gravy, waffles, omelets made to order, bagels and cream cheese, shrimp and Virginia ham, roast beef, and hash brown potatoes. There were gallons of fresh orange juice and some spicy tomato drinks. I stopped and took it all in with my eyes as a German tourist brushed by me hastily with his wife and two children in tow.

The tables were mostly full. By a window a group of Japanese men in business suits were speaking softly. At the next was a group of white women in jeans and windbreakers. One golden-haired woman was smoking a cigarette and nervously flicking it against the heavy glass ashtray. On one side of her plate, sitting on the linen tablecloth, was a VHF radio and a cellular phone. On the other was her leather cigarette case with turquoise and silver trim done in a pueblo design, including a small pouch for her butane lighter. The waitress brought that table three beers in long-necked bottles. She waved to the Chief of Police as he walked into the dining room. He was looking at us as he waved back at the waitress.

The German family sat down at their table. The children were fussing about who was going to sit closest to the window until the father gave them both a lecture and then set the timer on his Rolex watch.

The chief walked up to us and pulled a chair from the Germans' table. "Some night, huh, boys? What, you been camping?" He sat down and studied our appearance.

"No, Chief. I was just showing Cecil here the sights," Marcus answered and took a sip from his water glass. He left muddy prints dissolving down the sides.

"Well, I tell you I had quite a night. Christine finally stabbed her boyfriend."

"The heck she did?" Marcus spread his napkin on his lap.

"Yeah. I suppose it was just a matter of time." The chief played with the silverware.

"Kill him?" Marcus asked.

"Naw. Messy, though." The chief leaned back and faced me. "Well, you saw it, Cecil. I had to plug him up like that old Dutch boy and the dike. Messy. No, he's going to be okay. We stitched him up good enough to get him out to Anchorage by air ambulance. But I think Christine is going to have to stay with me for a while. Man, oh, man, I'm really tired. I just don't need any more of this. Say, did Mr. Ramirez ever find you, Marcus?"

A short dark-haired waiter came over and poured coffee. Marcus thanked him graciously, took a sip of coffee, and said to the chief, "No, he came by but we missed each other."

The chief declined his coffee and smiled at Marcus.

"Well, I heard he was still looking for you. You'll be leaving today, then, Cecil?"

"I'm not really sure, Chief," I said.

"I'd recommend it." The chief's tone had changed. His voice was low and had the weight of a slamming door. He added, "There's another storm behind this high pressure. You don't get out now, you might not get out."

I nodded and took another sip of my coffee. I tried to wipe the mud off my cheek.

Someone was breaking glassware in the corner of the room. We turned and saw a fisherman sitting alone, a broken water glass at his feet. He wore a gray hooded sweatshirt with the sleeves cut off at the shoulders, black pants, and old running shoes. He sat with his head propped up in one hand and a cigarette in the other. There was a beer bottle and a shot glass in front of him, and he had a long stare that I associated with a deeply profound moment of drunkenness. His eyebrows were arched and sad. His eyes were a stormy blue.

I buttered a bread stick with a heavy silver knife and watched the fisherman eyeing the room.

"Goddamn," he said, and his head wobbled out of his palm. "Goddamn, this can't be Dutch. This is fucking Seattle or something . . ."

Marcus leaned his massive forearms on the tablecloth and stared at me intently. "Chief, you're just in time because our friend Cecil here has never heard the story of the Centralia Massacre."

The chief sipped his water, looked absently at his watch and then at Marcus. The chief showed not a glimmer of interest. The drunken fisherman whooped and shouted like a rodeo rider. Marcus cleared his throat and set down his coffee cup with a certain formality. He said:

"It was 1919, just a year after the end of World War One. Democracy and commerce were the order of the day.

The international movement was starting to lose steam by factionalism, but the Wobblies were still strong in the woods. The eight-hour day. Clean blankets. Decent food. This wasn't just revolutionary rhetoric to the boys in the bunkhouses. This was something to get workers riled up about. Most of these boys went to work after the third grade so they could help feed their families. They didn't really know much about anarcho-syndicalism. They didn't care. Loggers would get killed or maimed every day and there was nowhere for them to go when they were hurt, no one to bury them. The bunkhouses were crowded, some fifty or sixty men to a cabin: the smell of sweat-soaked wool, liniment, and whiskey, the sounds of men coughing and bickering for more space near the one wood stove in the corner. The woods were a good place for radicals preaching discontent."

Marcus smiled at me. The fisherman whooped again and this time he slipped to one knee at the table. Everyone stared at him. The Japanese table considered him coolly and the German family gaped as if he might possibly be a wild animal worthy of a photograph. They stared silently like that until the father's timer went off and the children switched places near the window. When they did, the chief shifted in his chair and looked at his watch. Marcus continued on with his story.

"For the first anniversary of the Armistice, the American Legionnaires decided to put on a parade. To the veterans, the Wobs were all slackers and cowards. The Legion boys had some meetings at the Elks Hall before the parade and it was widely understood that the Wobbly Hall would have to be shut down. Closed for good.

"The Wobs had gotten wind of this plan, and went to a lawyer who had helped some of their members. The Wobblies wouldn't allow lawyers or anyone they saw as 'parasites' into the One Big Union. But they liked this lawyer all right. They asked him if they could defend their hall from attack.

The lawyer didn't even think about it. He told them they had a right to defend themselves. So the Wobs dug out their weapons.

"The night before the parade, the Wobblies had a meeting. There was an out-of-town speaker who gave a hell of a rousing speech but when the meeting turned to the defense of the hall, some of the boys spoke out against it. Hell, the hall had been trashed before. It was like a bonfire at a pep rally to the townspeople. But most of the boys already had their guns with them and they wanted to prove to the world that they were no cowards. The truth was they were scared shitless. Rumor had it the veterans were tired of the more symbolic trashing of the hall and were going to come after dark with clubs and guns. Most of the Wobs were either too young or too old to have been in the War. A couple of them had been in the Spruce Division to cut trees for the war effort. One was later rumored to have been a veteran of the bloody war in France, but that was never confirmed because the evening after the parade he was dead."

The waiter brought the drunken fisherman his check and said in a friendly tone that there were customers waiting for the table and he could take care of the bill right away unless, of course, there was anything else the man wanted to order.

The drunken fisherman stared up into the waiter's crisply starched shirtfront. His eyelids drooped as if he were about to fall asleep. He looked almost as if he were going to start crying.

"Yeah, fuck it," he slurred. "I'll get going. I better get a little further up the creek, you know?"

I had been staring at the fisherman so Marcus reached over and touched my elbow to get my attention.

"The Wobs wanted a fight. Some thought they should all stay right there in the hall when the vets came. Others thought that it would be most effective if they posted riflemen in the hotels across the street and a team of shooters up on Seminary Hill across the way. This way when the rush came, they could take out as many of the soldiers as possible in a crossfire. It's not really clear if they spelled this out to their lawyer but it was too late by that time. The boys had had enough and for the first time they were going to war.

"The day of the parade everybody was in place. The veterans assembled in uniform. None of the soldiers had weapons. None of them knew about the Wobbly riflemen in the hotels and on the hill. The main body of the parade had passed the hall and was turning around at the end of Trower Street when the Legionnaires halted in front of the Wobbly Hall. The head of the contingent called for the troops to close ranks because the parade was spreading out."

The fisherman stood up at that moment and clattered back against his table. The glass vase with its single rose shattered against his plate. The patrons in the restaurant stared at him with icy condescension. The fisherman looked around for a good fight but no one would fight him as long as they could ignore his noise. Finally, the waiter helped the drunk up the padded stairs to the polished wood desk where the cash register sat. Marcus kept on recounting the events of nearly eighty years ago.

"A commotion started. Nobody was really sure how. The leader of the contingent, a local boy, was shot in the chest, probably from above. No one agrees on where the boy was standing, if he was marching or breaking into the hall, but it is pretty clear he was facing whoever shot him. His name was Warren Grimm."

I stopped Marcus from going on. "Wait a minute. Warren Grimm was a Legionnaire shot down in 1919?"

Marcus had his friendly smile on and he winked at me, then went right on. "Another Legionnaire was leaning around the corner to try and make out where the shooting was coming from. He was shot through the brain.

"Wesley Everest had stayed inside the Wobbly Hall with his pistol. Wesley was one of the hottest and most doctrinaire Wobblies in the area. Wesley had been a soldier. He was a vet. As the Legionnaires rushed the hall, the plate glass windows shattered and they broke the door off the frame. Wesley Everest fired his pistol, and he must have known that the Wobbly plan was going badly for he was the first to run out the back of the hall and head for the river. As Wesley Everest ran down the alley, he shot at two unarmed men in uniform. He killed one of them. The Legionnaires chased him out into the river. By the time the mob got him to the jail downtown, Wesley had killed one more of them and he had a rope around his neck. He screamed at the crowd, 'You boys don't have the guts to lynch a man in broad daylight.' There was some discussion apparently about just when was the best time to lynch a man, and then they threw Wesley into the jail with anyone else they could find.

"That night, the police and vigilantes filled that jail right up. Anyone who was even rumored to be a Wobbly was rounded up and thrown inside. By nightfall, federal troops were on the way from Tacoma to restore order. But hours before they could arrive, someone cut the lines and the town lost power. The lights went off and a mob rushed the jail. They pulled Everest out of his cell and they hanged him.

"They dragged Wesley Everest's corpse back into the jail and flopped him on the cement floor for all the boys to see. A nineteen-year-old kid named Loren Roberts was the first one to talk. Later the Wobblies said Loren Roberts was crazy, but that night I think the kid was just looking for any way out. They didn't have to use a rubber hose on him. He had been in the cell listening to the crowd outside. He had seen the lights go out and the mob take Everest and the mob bring him back. Loren Roberts told that mob who had done the shooting and why."

The chief looked at me and smiled as he made a show

out of looking at his wristwatch again. "You know, I'm sure Mr. Younger is finding this very interesting, but really—"

"Just a little more here, Chief. This next part is really going to perk up our private eye."

I could hear the waiters arguing with the drunken fisherman out near the entrance to the dining room. Marcus leaned in closer, his dark head filling my vision like a mountain as he said softly, "Loren Roberts had been up on Seminary Hill with Burt Bland whose nickname was Curly. And there was another kid named Ole Hanson." Marcus sighed and his breath was warm and bitter with the smell of coffee. "Loren swore that a man named Davis was the shooter in the Hotel. But Ole Hanson was the shooter on the hillside."

"What happened to Ole Hanson?" I asked Marcus.

"Davis and Hanson were never captured. There were reports all over the country. Davis and Hanson were seen from Montesano to Seattle to Bangkok. There was a report that both were lynched that same night, and another that Ole was killed and buried in a field in Oakville."

Marcus smiled at me. Lights were dancing in his dark eyes. "But the truth is those two workers were never found."

A young uniformed police officer stood in the entrance of the dining room and he nodded to the chief and the chief smiled and nodded back at him with a trace of irritation as if the young cop was late. But the chief turned back to Marcus and smiled. "Yeah, these workers just keep getting exploited, too." The chief was grinning over the lip of his coffee cup. He set the cup in the white saucer. "You know, there were days here in Dutch in the late seventies when there was so much money the poor boys just had to piss it away. The prices were up and the crabs were fighting to get into the pots. A kid who worked twenty days could make sixty or seventy thousand dollars. Kids would charter Lear jets to Seattle. Couple of drunks had a contest to see who could throw their gold watches the farthest out into the bay."

There was a disturbance up front. Not loud or angry, but a slur of friendly voices, then laughter and the churning of the cash register.

The waiter came to our table and poured orange juice with a deferential smile and a soft "hi" to the chief. The chief took a sip and went on with his story. "Of course, cocaine was real big then. There is something about making big money at dangerous and repetitive work that makes cocaine very attractive. A nice buzz lets you keep working. Don't you think that's true, Cecil?"

I lifted the heavy silver fork in my hand and drew a pattern on the tablecloth with the tines. I spoke down into the design. "Well, I know you've checked my record, Chief, so I suppose you're asking my expert opinion. Cocaine makes everybody think they're movie stars. Even if you're sliming fish. At least that's what I've been told." I smiled at the chief as the alarm went off on the German's Rolex and the kids traded places again.

The chief asked Marcus in a friendly voice, "Now, you don't sell cocaine over there at your club, do you?" He was grinning broadly.

Marcus, who was smiling in return, said, "Chief, I think you are really obsessed. You should see someone. You know I'm committed to sobriety. Drugs are a tool of the oppressors." Marcus spoke with a joking tone and tried to lightly bump his fist against the chief's shoulder.

The chief recoiled from the tap. "I just thought I'd ask, because, you know, an awful lot of junkies come in and out of there. I mean, any night of the week, say, tonight, I could go in there and find a couple of bindles of powder, don't you think? You know, you two look so good together. I can see why you're going on this trip together."

"Together?" Marcus asked calmly.

"Yeah, well, that's what I thought. But there's no reason we can't finish our meal first. Then I'll drive you both over to the airport."

Marcus, not smiling now, looked down at his hands. Then over his shoulder at the young uniformed officer leaning against the steam table talking to a waitress.

The waiter returned and stood silently with his order pad. "I'll need to stop off and get some things," Marcus told the chief quietly.

"Sure, sure, I'll swing you by." The chief looked up at the waiter and said, "We'll all have the brunch buffet, please, James."

James nodded and gestured toward the steam table as if he were leading the way to the promised land.

At the buffet, the chief loaded his plate with fresh fruit and bacon, hash brown potatoes, and a slice of broccoli quiche. He looked down at the plate as he said, "You know, it's funny, isn't it? James, there, the waiter. He used to be a doctor back in Vietnam. Now he's here with his family and there's three generations of them working in the kitchen. You've got to kind of wonder why he and his family would want to come to this country, it being so corrupt and exploitative and all." The Chief of Police nudged Marcus, who was putting a strawberry covered in bittersweet chocolate on his plate. Marcus looked up, irritated. The chief added, "But James doesn't have to worry about police repression anymore, does he?" Then he laughed his long nasal whinny that caused everyone in the place to smile to themselves.

We ate until we were full and then went back for sampling tastes. I was eating a piece of chocolate cheesecake with a smothering of raspberries and Marcus was finishing his coffee and apricot torte when David Ramirez shoved past James and stood above our table. I felt a chill as if I were standing at the bottom of a cliff at sunset.

The chief looked up at him and took another bite of his cheese Danish.

"These men are in my custody. So I'm sorry, you won't be able to talk to them. Of course, if you're thinking of making a public disturbance I can have one of my officers take you into custody, too," the chief said as politely as a flight attendant.

David Ramirez shook his shaggy head. There was another clattering near the front of the restaurant and the drunk fisherman lurched into one of the steam tables. He saved it from tipping over but had to hold on to the hot plate underneath with his bare hands. I could see where it was burning into the calloused flesh on his palms but he didn't seem to mind. He set the steam table to rights and whooped again as if he had a fish on. Then he disappeared around the corner.

I turned my attention back to the table and saw David Ramirez walking toward the door.

"Right, then," the chief said, and he wiped his mouth carefully with a napkin, then looked at his watch. "You guys set? We better be going." He waved to get James's attention.

James came down the stairs and over to our table and bowed slightly. "That's all right, Chief. It's been taken care of."

"James, you know I can't do that. I can't accept gifts. I'll just take care of it."

James's eyes widened with an amused kind of panic. He shook his head vigorously. "No. No. No. Not me. Not me. The man with the beers and the tequila. The drunk man. He bought everybody's breakfast. He said he wanted to buy everybody's breakfast. He had money. Cash money. The manager said he could do it. So he buys your breakfast, too."

"Jesus." The chief took a toothpick, unwrapped it, and looked around the crowded restaurant. "That's got to be what, eight, nine hundred bucks?"

James smiled at us and spread his hands wide with palms up. "Money. What's it for? For a man like that. What's it for?"

"Beats the hell out of me." The chief sucked on his toothpick and headed toward the door. Then he doubled back.

"Did he take care of your tip?"

James nodded and bowed almost involuntarily. "Oh, yes. A very good tip. Thank you, Chief."

The chief stood back and allowed us to walk ahead of him. Just out the door that led to the hotel lobby sat one of his deputies. The deputy was drinking a cup of coffee, talking to one of the housemaids. He put his coffee cup down quickly when we walked out.

"All right, then." The chief clapped his hands together as if it were the beginning of a brand-new day. "Let's get these guys to the airplane!"

Marcus and I shouldered around the drunk fisherman, who was wobbling on his feet trying unsuccessfully to light the wrong end of his filter-tipped cigarette. "Thanks for the breakfast, comrade," I said in a hearty voice, and the fisherman looked up at me as if I were disturbing his sleep. "Kiss my ass, punk," he mumbled.

"You gotta love this revolution," I said to Marcus.

"Fuck you, Younger," he said. Then the chief put his hands on both of our shoulders.

"Now come on, boys. Let's watch the language. Watch the language. There are ladies present."

The chief had his deputy escort us through airport security and all the way onto the plane. The deputy opened the overhead storage so I could put my muddy pack on top of the neatly folded airline blankets. Marcus had been able to change his clothes in town so when he handed me his coat to put overhead he asked that I not put it near my pack. The deputy helped Marcus fish out the buckle of his seat belt. We were up toward the front of the plane. David Ramirez got a seat toward the rear. The deputy stayed in the cabin of the plane until the attendants were ready to close the rear door and pull the stairs away. Then the deputy tapped David Ramirez on the shoulder and said something to him. Ramirez looked forward and shook his head without changing expression.

The water was a haze of churning waves. The wind was boiling against the Aleutian Islands like a wild river. The plane charged the end of the runway and pulled up like a rising fly ball, then banked against the face of the mountain. I had my eyes closed as Marcus started whispering to me.

"Daddy Ramirez isn't going to do anything during the flight, and I imagine the chief's friends will meet us in Anchorage."

The plane lurched to one side as it cleared the mountain. I deduced this from the shift of my internal organs. Marcus, who apparently was oblivious to gut-crushing G-forces, kept talking as if we were in the stateroom of a riverboat.

"By tonight they'll have a warrant and the club will be closed for the next month."

"I thought you didn't allow drugs or guns," I said through my clenched teeth.

"Well, that's true. But I think if you look hard enough anywhere in America you're going to find drugs or guns."

"Is that a denial or an explanation?" I asked, feeling a little peevish with the big man now that he was strapped in.

The plane had leveled out and was bursting up through the next layer of fast-moving weather. I opened my eyes and saw Marcus staring at me with a look of genuine confusion.

"Just what are you up to, Younger?" He was looking at me as if I had just set my clothes on fire.

"I need to talk to Simon Delaney." The plane lurched

again and I felt the contents of my lower intestine moving the wrong direction. "Where is he?"

"And I told you, Mr. Younger. Simon wants William Flynn's money."

"How much does he want?" I heard the flight attendants start to rattle the latched bulkheads in the plane's galley. I fished in my pockets to see if there were any Xanax in with the lint and loose change.

"He wants all of it," Marcus said.

I pulled my hand out of my soggy pockets and there was nothing but lint and a fine blue paste left from my melted medication. "Well, you're going to have to talk to William Flynn about that," I said as I licked my fingers.

Marcus stretched back in his seat. The plane dropped precipitously. Someone shrieked and a baby began crying inconsolably. Marcus looked up at the ceiling of the jet. "Yeah. Okay. I'll go see the old man with you. Maybe we can work a deal. I bought a ticket for Seattle, but I can stop over in Sitka. Then we can go on down and see where Simon is . . . if the old man comes up with the money," he said as the flight attendant rolled the cart past. He paid for four small bottles of bourbon. He put them in my lap.

"Is that all right with you?" he asked, although I was only paying attention to the shiny bottles. They sat like a tiny pair of binoculars in my lap. The plane lurched again and the frames of the seats creaked and the flight attendant stumbled, flopping down into my lap. I could smell her cosmetics and as I was helping her regain her composure I felt some type of foundation garment under her uniform. The pilot's voice came soothingly over the speakers. He asked everyone to return to their seats and buckle up. The flight attendant apologized and squeezed my shoulder in a touching gesture that convinced me we were all about to die in a molten fireball of aviation gas and fused aluminum.

She smiled, apologized again, and gave me two more

bottles of bourbon. "Yeah. That's all right," I said as I opened the first of the six.

I was both heavy with guilt and giddy with morbid joie de vivre by the time we had to change planes in Anchorage. As expected, airport security walked with us to meet our next plane. Marcus bought me another drink at the bar even though it meant our whole parade had to go through security. David Ramirez walked slowly behind us like a stalking bear, but he kept well back. I don't remember seeing him as we got on the next plane, the one down the coast to Juneau and Sitka. I was buckling my belt and wondering when flight service would begin. Marcus put my bag up in the overhead. He glanced down at me with a bothered look.

"Shit." He looked toward the front of the plane and started nudging the man who was trying to get past him. "I left my jacket on the other plane, Cecil. Hey, if she asks, just get me soda for after takeoff. I'll run down to the gate and be right back. You okay, man? You look sick or something."

"No. No. I'm all right really, just tired, a little sick to my stomach maybe, scared or something. I'm sorry," I told him, closed my eyes and pushed my seat back.

"Okay," he said in the distance. "I'll be right back."

A few minutes later the doors closed and the plane pushed back. The seat next to mine was empty. The flight attendant yelled at me as I stood up and opened the overhead. She unbuckled her own seat belt and came charging down the aisle as I threw the blankets and pillows on the passengers around me. She put both her hands on my shoulders to push me down into my seat, but I stayed upright staring at the overhead compartment. All that was there was Marcus's damp wool jacket. I looked up and down the fuselage. David Ramirez, Marcus, and my backpack with William Flynn's money were all missing.

Soon there was a large male flight attendant with a calming voice pressing his thumb into my left bicep with such force I had to wipe the tears from my eyes before I rebuckled my seat belt.

I got off the plane in Sitka carrying Marcus's wool coat. It felt as big and heavy as a buffalo robe. He had taken his wallet and all of the pockets were empty. I tried each one twice. I gave up on the third go-through of the inside lining. Then I rubbed it to my face, smelling the damp wool and the faint trace of the disappeared Marcus.

My head was starting to hurt and my stomach churned from the whiskey. I bought breath mints and gum from the vending machine, then started to walk home in the rain.

I was getting used to being soaking wet by the time I walked through my front door. So used to it, I was considering living outdoors the rest of my life. I heard voices upstairs when I walked in and felt grateful for that. Upstairs it seemed like there was a crowd of tiny people in and around my kitchen. There was an extra leaf placed in the table and there were backs and elbows of extra small children who were shoveling things into their mouths. Todd had his mouth full but waved as I came in. Priscilla was standing at the stove stirring a pot with a wooden spoon and a couple of dark-eyed children were walking back to the table with heaping bowls of ice cream. Jane Marie came around the corner carrying soggy bags of berries.

"Oh, God, Cecil. I'm glad you're back. The chest freezer broke down this morning. I'm trying to do something with all the food. I'm going to take any of it that hasn't thawed completely up the street to Jake and Mary's freezer. Priscilla is making jam and I invited the kids in to eat all the ice cream."

Young Bob smiled up at me and waved his prosthetic hand gaily. He had a clown's face of smeared ice cream. Next to Todd sat two dark-eyed children. They had black hair and as I looked at them they tried to sink smaller into their chairs, worried, I suppose, that I was going to do something about the ice cream.

"Who are those kids?"

Jane Marie was washing off the red huckleberries in a stainless steel bowl. "This is Anita and Thomas, Cecil. They are . . . Mr. Ramirez's grandchildren. You remember? They are staying with their old neighbors up the street. I thought they might help out with the ice cream eating crisis."

Both children grinned at me but did not go back to eating the ice cream until I smiled at them and said hello. Then they dove in. I walked over to Jane Marie by the sink.

"Christ. What is this, Ellis Island or something?"

"Cecil, the freezer broke. You want me to waste all that food? Besides, where do you get off making such an ugly comment?"

"I'm sorry . . . I just . . . wasn't expecting to see them, that's all."

"God, you look terrible." She looked at me. My pants were stiff with greasy mud that had dried on the plane but now was slick again with the rain. My hair spiked down my skull.

"Any luck with finding Simon Delaney?" she asked and flicked some berry leaves into a compost bucket.

"No," I said and nothing more.

I felt a tug on my pants leg. I looked down: Angela's two children were holding their empty bowls out, setting what must have been some kind of land speed record for ice cream consumption. The boy, who was very thin and seemed to have an unusually large head, was pulling on my leg.

"My mother's dead, you know," he informed me in a soft voice.

"I know," I said. I shifted on my feet. I fought back the urge to start tickling him just to change the subject.

"Are you sad that my mom's dead?" he asked.

His big sister nudged him. "Of course he's sad,

dummy. Just get some more ice cream." She took him by the arm and after saying "excuse me" very nicely she steered her brother over to Priscilla, who spooned out some more soupy Neapolitan with the flavors all swirled together.

"Do you know what's wrong with the freezer?" I asked Jane Marie, thinking I was shifting the subject away from mortality.

"It's not cold," she answered and she kissed me.

"Mmm. Minty," she said, squinting at me. Worried. I turned away from her quickly and left the room.

The freezer was indeed warm. It sat in the corner of the storage room like a rotting corpse, the rich smell of red meat coming up from its lid. I opened it tentatively. Months of food. Berries from the hill behind the graveyard, venison from Kruzof Island, halibut from my private fishing hole in Hayward Strait, coho salmon from near Biorka Island, sockeye from Necker Bay, bricks of butter probably from Wisconsin or someplace, a pizza a friend shipped to us from Chicago in dry ice, tubs of ice cream, bags of frozen vegetables, even a bottle of Bombay gin I had forgotten about years ago. Everything seemed limp and soggy, even the bottle of gin. I felt suddenly very depressed looking at it. I didn't have enough money for a new freezer and I wasn't smart enough to fix this one. I felt like an amateur investor seeing all of my savings flutter off a rooftop.

Jane Marie walked in behind me and closed the door. "Cecil . . . ," she said tentatively. I could hear her apprehension. "Have you been drinking?"

"Yeah," I said flatly, and looked down into the freezer. A cracked carton of raspberry juice was dripping down onto a bag of french fries, the juice smearing red and pooling in the creases.

"Are you drunk?"

"No. No, baby. I'm not drunk. I'm just . . . not very good at what I do."

I felt her arms around me. She hugged me close. "You're good at what you do for me." Her body was strong. Her fingers laced around my chest. "Don't drink anymore. It won't make anything better." I felt her cheek press against my back. "And you'll lose me. I couldn't stand that."

"Okay. I guess," I said with conviction. I turned around and she kissed me hard, backing me up against the freezer.

Over her shoulder I could see Angela's children. They had opened the door and were holding their ice cream bowls and watching us.

"Hey, guys," I said and ducked out from under Jane Marie. I bent down onto my haunches so that I could be more nearly at their eye level. "Did you kids like the ice cream?" They nodded vigorously. "I need to talk to you a minute."

"Cecil," Jane Marie said sternly. "Don't."

The kids heard something in Jane Marie's voice and started to back away from me. I quickly stood up and whispered to Jane Marie. "Listen, I need to know what happened on the day their mom died."

"Cecil, for Christ's sake. They don't need this now."

"Momma took her little gun." The little girl dropped her ice cream bowl. Her voice was flat. She stared at the empty bowl.

Jane Marie leaned down to her and wrapped her in her arms. "You don't have to talk about it, honey." And she lifted the child up, carrying her out of the room.

Her brother stood there staring into his empty bowl. He would not look at me, but he mumbled, "She thinks Simon is going to kill us."

"I won't let him kill you," I said very slowly and calmly, praying to myself that it was true.

A single tear dropped into the boy's ice cream bowl. "Will I go to hell if I tell a secret?" Thomas asked. That was easy for me and I quickly said, "No. You won't go to hell."

"Simon was home. He didn't get on the ferryboat. He said if we told anybody they would split us up. Put us in different homes. Then we'd be alone."

I scooped the tiny boy up into my arms and took him back out into the kitchen. "You promise I won't go to hell or get in trouble?" I could feel his breath on my face as he spoke.

"Yes. I promise," I said and set him down at the table.

"Have you told anyone else about this?" I asked Thomas.

He was twisting his fingers together, looking over in the direction of his sister without meeting her eyes.

"We told Grandpa. When he came here. That first morning. I told him."

Sometimes I think I've been a fuck-up for so long that I don't really know the difference between caution and cowardice. It is true I'm afraid of almost everything. But one of the things I'm most truly afraid of is the scorn of those people truly deserving of love. So I knew without a doubt that I had to do whatever it took to find Simon Delaney, if for nothing else than to protect this skinny little kid with the salty ice cream dish.

I turned to Jane Marie. "I'm sorry. I won't ask any questions but I've got to go look for Simon Delaney. Do you have any of those free tickets the airline gave us after they screwed up that trip?" Jane Marie would not look at me but stood at the sink holding a limp-looking chicken, examining it as if she were a veterinarian.

"Yeah, I do," she said and her voice was still icy. "I have two of them. They're on your desk. You can take both."

"I just need one."

She put the chicken back to one side and didn't look at me as she spoke. "Well, actually, Cecil, you need two."

"Why two?" I bent down, trying without success to catch her eye. She wouldn't look at me.

"I'm headed out on a research trip and the Social Services people say that you have to be more responsible for Todd. Particularly because he's not working anymore."

"So he has to come with me to Centralia?" I asked, staring at her as if she had just revealed herself as a space alien.

"Yes," she said and nodded her head decisively.

"I can't take Todd with me, Janie. Hell, you know he's never even been out of Alaska. He's forty-two years old. He's never been south of Ketchikan. I can't take him. I don't have the money. He would hate the trip. He would hate it down there. Can't he go with you?" I was out of breath.

"Are you finished?" Her arms were folded. She took a deep breath and started speaking. Her voice was pinched now.

"No, he can't come with me, Cecil. You are his guardian. You are responsible for him. Not me. Besides, there is no more room on my boat. I'm taking a camera crew and three students as it is."

"Can't you put it off for a few days?" I pleaded.

"Goddamnit, Cecil." She slammed down the lid of the freezer. "Don't come in here after being gone and leaving me with this house and this stupid freezer." Her whole body shook. "Don't come back here sulking and stinking of . . . of . . . breath mints, then complain about your responsibilities! I'm not your mother."

"Well, how the fuck was I supposed to know that. You both sound the same," I said to her back as it was disappearing out the door.

I saw a blue coat flipping over the banister at the same time I heard her feet on the stairs. "Take care of your own damn freezer," were the words I heard clearly. There were others that came after but the slamming door must have muffled them.

In the kitchen, Priscilla was putting on her coat slowly. She walked to the rack by the stove and took three children's coats and turned to the kids at the table. "Come on, young ones. It's time to go." All three children groaned and shoveled the last ice cream into their mouths.

"The jam's boiling on the stove," Priscilla told me. "You might want to stir it. If you're sober enough."

The kids walked past me and their silence was filled with a sort of condensed recrimination. Their rain boots clattered on the steps like a troop of hangmen. Thomas waved at me and his expression burned with trust. I waved back weakly.

Toddy pushed back from his ice cream. He had a chocolate mustache. His glasses were crooked from where they had broken at the bridge years ago. The gray tape curled up off the thin metal. He had a book open and was listening to a tape on his little boom box next to the table. For the first time since I arrived I realized that there was something coming from the boom box speakers.

A man's voice. Very deep and sonorous, speaking slowly and clearly: *Finding the right words to use in English takes practice and experience. Don't be timid. Go ahead and use the new words we have learned in this audiocassette series. Only by experience will you gain the confidence to use your newfound vocabulary. Let's turn to page twenty-six of your workbook and circle the definitions for these words: "Criterion" . . . "Calamity" . . . "Commodious" . . .*

I walked across the room to Todd. "Can you turn that off, buddy?" Todd reached over and touched the stop button.

"Would you like to fly down to Seattle with me tomorrow, Todd?"

He did not answer but stared at me for a long moment. His brow was furrowed. He licked the chocolate from his upper lip. He sat up straight in his chair and still he didn't say a thing.

I continued, "Well. I've got some tickets. We can go together. What do you say?"

He stared at me and his eyes glittered with tears.

"Do I have to?" he asked softly, biting his lower lip.

"Yes," I said, irritated by the pathetic sight of him. "You do."

Todd took a deep breath and ran his hands down the front of his pants legs. He thought a moment, collecting himself. "Will this be an extended journey, Cecil?" There was only trust in his voice.

"Yes, Todd," I said, slumping down in my own chair and wringing my hands together. "I think this may be an extended journey."

Chapter Seven

It was true. Todd had never been outside of southeastern Alaska. His father had worked the logging camps and his mother was a schoolteacher. He had been in Ketchikan, Sitka, and the camps of Prince of Wales Island. Once, he had been to the docks in Juneau on his dad's fishing boat, but he never went far from the boat, worrying his father might unexpectedly leave without him.

Todd knew about the rest of the world from books and television. He had a wonderful memory. He could tell you detailed facts about the geography of Antarctica. He knew the social rituals of gibbon monkeys and he could recount the histories of several European monarchies. In short, the larger world was a collage in his head composed from a jumble of selections he'd made in his reading, but the *actual* world, the world he was soaked in and built from, was constant. The real world has salt water on one side, steep mountains on the other, and rain falling down on everything.

I'm sure the panic started to set in when we left the plane and walked down the terminal concourse in Seattle.

This was the largest covered area Todd had ever seen: hallways like roads with walls on both sides, black men driving whirring electric go-carts, people in church clothes walking swiftly just one way or the other, not looking at each other, their heels sparking on linoleum. Todd had never seen this. Never seen people sluiced down hallways. He looked around wildly. There was a sculpture hanging from the ceiling depicting a kayak with dozens of oars sweeping out on each side. Each oar hung by several silver wires and the oars did not move. I suppose the sculpture was intended to suggest motion through water, but it hung stock-still high in the air above a piece of polished stone. There was dust on the skin of the boat. The silver wires glinted like knives. There were mirrored figures carved into the side of its hull. A telephone. A bear. Stars. It wasn't real, yet there it was: an imaginary boat floating in actual air. The larger world was about to unfold to Todd just like that. He clutched his dictionary, stared straight ahead, and walked quickly down the concourse at my side.

I hadn't emptied my checking account but I had split the difference. I had $175.00 in cash in my pocket and had written a check for $50.00 to Jake and Mary if they could save any of the food in my freezer and look after Todd's dog Wendall. Mary showed up in the morning before we went to the airport with garbage bags and dance music tapes to play while making jam. I never heard from Jane Marie.

We had no baggage so we went to find the city bus that could take us into the city. There we could transfer to a commercial bus for Centralia.

Todd knew to stick close to me. Concerning getting lost, I had told him this: If we get separated, stay put and I'll always find you. If you are in danger and have to move from where you are, go someplace that feels safe. Stay there. Ask for help.

If his first sight of public art work had confused

him, his emergence into a big-city bus station caused him to grip his dictionary to his chest even tighter. I sat him down on one of the molded plastic chairs attached in rows to a chrome bar that was bolted to the floor. I told him to wait while I bought our tickets. The air smelled of diesel exhaust, ammonia, cigarettes, and fabric soaked through with sweat. I stood in line behind a man holding a cardboard box tied with rope, which he tugged along as if it were a burro as he yelled over to his children sleeping on the plastic benches. There was a Great Dane in a cage near the ticket counter and a white woman fed him pieces of her hamburger through the wire door. Her hands were smeared with mustard. The dog's great pink tongue lapped against the wire as she held her hand up for him to clean. An old white woman in a flowered housedress and bedroom slippers nudged a grocery cart filled with lumpy plastic bags into the terminal. She had a bandage on her shin that was damp, the hint of blood like a lipstick stain under the second layer of gauze. A black security guard in a uniform that was too small for him told the old woman to take the cart outside and she started shouting, pointing her finger at him like a gun. I heard her voice rise in urgency. She said something about cops and invisible wires "connecting everybody." I looked away, then I heard her scream. When I looked back she was gone. So was her grocery cart. The security guy was walking back from the swinging doors tugging his jacket down over his stomach. A man in a torn green coat asked me for money to buy his fare to Tacoma. He was a veteran, he said. I shrugged, said "I'm sorry," and without a change in tone he turned his attention to the woman behind me. A black soldier sat smoking a cigarette in a plastic chair with a TV mounted on its arm. A young girl kept trying to ease up into his lap to see what was on, but the screen was blank and the soldier brushed her down.

I bought our tickets and moved around the counter

to look through the concourse gate to make sure I understood where we had to go to catch our bus. I opened the glass door and the security guard touched my arm and told me they weren't calling for any buses right then and I'd have to wait. His expression was flat, his tone calm, not threatening or unfriendly but tired, as if he almost didn't have the energy to get the words out.

The door opened suddenly and the security guard turned, his eyes wide now, his posture erect. The bag lady stepped through the door and flung a paper cup full of warm yellow liquid over the guard. "I didn't put you in my movie, motherfucker!" she shrieked. "What are you doing in my goddamn movie?"

The security guy took most of it, but I was hit with urine down my right sleeve and on my cheek and neck. The guard lunged out the door and I walked to the bathroom.

A white soldier was shaving at the sink. His bristly scalp showed like bone in the fluorescent lights. He held an old-fashioned shaving brush and he soaped his face lovingly while smoking a cigarette. He was standing in his undershirt with his uniform coat hanging on the towel dispenser. He was humming "Chattanooga Choo-Choo." The bathroom was quiet as a dream. We were alone there, and as I soaked my sleeve in the sink and wiped my neck and collar with damp paper towels I considered staying in there the rest of the afternoon, maybe even borrowing the soldier's brush and razor so I could shave, too. The soldier finished up, packed his shaving kit into his bag, and walked out. Two men came in and started rolling a joint.

I left. A Seattle policeman was talking to the security guy, who shook his head from side to side as he told his story. The cop had his notebook out but didn't write a thing. The old lady with the empty cup was gone.

I turned back to the row of chairs and Toddy was not

there. Bile churned in my stomach. I scanned the four corners of the room. He was not there. I yanked on the policeman's sleeve and he asked me to wait. A black man wearing a
gray suit guided his tweed suitcase up the line with his foot. I
asked about a big white man holding a dictionary and looking
lost and the black man shook his head slowly, sympatheti-
cally, not seeming surprised by the strangeness of my description. I went to every corner of the bus station, took every new
view down the stairs or around the corners. Around every
blind corner I expected to see Todd, but I didn't. I ducked
back into the bathroom and threw up.

I ran outside onto the steps of the bus station. I
saw rows of warehouses, utility poles covered with layers of
bright, tattered handbills. Cars eased past quietly on their
radial tires, but he was gone. Everything I saw, everything I
heard, was not him.

My panic was making me weak and I started across
the ridge of the hill toward salt water, feeling sick to my stomach. I pushed my way past people walking in the same direction and I stood on my toes to scan the crowd, then I took
off running. The air had the metallic taste of smog and salt.
I asked a woman who was selling gold chains on the top of a
briefcase if she'd seen Todd. She just shook her head as she
dangled chains on her forearm. I asked a kid dressed in black
with purple hair. He looked all around where we were standing, as if Todd might have fallen out of my pocket. Then he
said, "No." I ran toward the waterfront, past espresso stands
and street musicians. A Vietnamese woman selling T-shirts
with cartoon characters ironed on their fronts shook her head
sadly as I asked.

I passed the lobby of an old hotel, then turned back
and pushed through the door. The air inside was fragrant
with coffee and leather. The big room was dominated by a
huge Oriental vase with colorful sprays of blue and yellow
flowers. I didn't know the names of the flowers but they had

the presence of a waterfall in the quiet glen of that lobby. A young man in a bell captain's uniform walked by me silently. An older white woman wearing a red blazer and gold necklace asked me if I was all right. I told her that I had lost my friend. She shook her head and suggested I call the police. I could smell her perfume. I saw her fiddle with the heavy gold earring on her left ear and for some reason I believed that she must know where Toddy was. She offered to help and I asked her if she had seen a middle-aged man with broken glasses and a dictionary. Then she told me that I should wait in one place for my friend to find me, and she raised her thin arm to look at her gold wristwatch and I realized I had been dismissed. I bolted out the door into the rattle of the street.

When I rounded the stairs by the public market I looked out toward the waters of Puget Sound. Before I recognized anything, I was struck by a calming feeling: It was the crazy, almost narcotic effect of damp air.

To the north a squall was sweeping down the sound. It was a silvery sheet that blanketed out the Olympic Mountains. Gulls wheeled in front of the wind, and even from this far away I could smell rain blending with the smells of the market: fish and scented candles. The closer the squall came, the stronger the smell of rain grew. This weather had come from Alaska. Down by the aquarium he was standing, rocking back and forth. A crone of a woman with strings of gray hair spilling out of her hooded sweatshirt hovered near him. She moved her hands over his coat, dipping her fingers into his coat pockets, murmuring, "Okay, hon? Are you okay?" Todd was cradling his dictionary. His eyes were tightly closed. The crone fished his wallet out of his raincoat and I grabbed her wrists.

"Hey, back the fuck off, man! I'll call a cop. I'll call a cop if you think you're going to rape me. I'll call a cop," she hissed.

"I just wanted to thank you for helping my friend. I wanted to offer you a reward." I tried to say it soothingly.

Recognizing my voice, Todd opened his eyes, but when he saw the crone he closed them again.

I gave her five bucks and she walked quickly away, disappearing into the alley at the foot of the hill. Todd opened his eyes. I hugged him and the squall closed in around us.

"I became extraordinarily anxious, Cecil. I considered the possibility that I was . . . claustrophobic." He broke away and would not face me. He held his head up to the rain as it started to fall. His glasses streaked and began to fog. "I'm sorry," he murmured.

"That's okay, buddy. We don't have to take the bus." I said it without much conviction.

The rain had stopped abruptly and the traffic surged past us like a stampede of mechanical bison. Rushing noise without rhythm. I stood by the sign that said NO HITCH-HIKING BEYOND THIS POINT and held my thumb out. Todd stood next to me with his bag around his shoulder and his dictionary in his hands, looking happy and relieved.

My wool coat still smelled bad and I sniffed at the sleeve as each prospective ride passed us by, worrying that somehow they had smelled me. Toddy was wearing an old tan raincoat that someone had bought so he could wear it to a funeral. We were two middle-aged white men traveling together who looked as if we didn't have fifty cents between us. We looked either like homosexual serial killers or like bait for homosexual serial killers. I wasn't sure what I wanted to look more like, so I put my collar up and ran my fingers through my thinning hair and hoped I looked more like Jack Nicholson.

After forty-five minutes I was shocked to see a Volvo station wagon with a handsome young couple pull over on the shoulder of the road. The driver turned around and waved us toward him.

I opened the back door and Todd piled in, sliding to the other side of the car, holding his dictionary very carefully, as if it might break. I jumped in and slammed the door.

"Hey, fellas, how far ya going?" the young man in tortoiseshell glasses asked.

"We're on our way to Centralia. Thanks for stopping," I answered.

The woman sat rigid in the front seat. I leaned forward and could see she was wearing an expensive Norwegian-style cardigan sweater and she had a pearl barrette in her shiny brown hair. "Really. Thanks for stopping. We were waiting quite a while," I told them and the woman shrank back as if she thought I might be carrying the Ebola virus. She held up her face to shield herself. I sat back in the leather seats.

The man spoke, watching me through his rearview mirror. "Well, we can't get you all the way to Centralia. We're just going to—" The woman slammed him with her elbow.

"Hugh!" she coughed out. "What do you think you're doing?"

Hugh looked at her with a sour expression, clearly angry. But he said nothing as we pulled out onto the freeway, smoothly into the middle lane.

Finally he said, "Well, we'll get you close." We rode in silence.

Toddy opened his dictionary and started thumbing through the pages. The thin young woman spun around in the seat.

"My God, what's that?" she shrilled.

"A dictionary," Toddy said calmly.

"It's not a Bible, is it? Just don't start reading the Bible."

Hugh accelerated up past sixty-five. Linda was sitting forward in her bucket seat. "They start reading the Bible in prison. It's how they conceal their rage," Linda was muttering out of the side of her mouth.

"Oh, for God's sake, Linda," the driver said. "He said it was a dictionary."

"What? You *read* a dictionary?" she snapped.

"No . . . I guess I just look things up," Todd offered lamely. "But I do have certain passages of the Bible committed to memory." Todd took a deep breath and I could tell he was about to launch into the Sermon on the Mount. I elbowed him.

"Ix-nay on the Ible-bay," I whispered through my own clenched teeth. Toddy looked at me confused and then started riffling through the dictionary.

"You have to excuse her, guys. You see, she's anxious about picking up hitchhikers." Hugh smiled up at us again through the mirror. "I had a heck of a time convincing her to let me pick you up."

Linda let out an exasperated grunt.

"But I told her, I thumbed around all over the country. Especially back when I was in law school. I owe the road a lot of dues. You know what I mean?"

Linda was fuming. She spoke this time without any worry of concealment. "Oh, you always do this. You always do this. Particularly if there are any other men around."

"Men around?" Hugh glanced back at us skeptically in his mirror with that "she's probably having her period" knowing look.

"Oh, yes," Linda pushed on. "You can lie up in bed and think you're having a heart attack and ask me to call nine-one-one like a dope and cry and whine about imaginary chest pains."

"Indigestion," Hugh snapped.

"Whatever." Linda sat back and stared down the

road. "But if you get around any men, oh no, you turn into Indiana Jones or something. The great adventurer of the Woodstock nation. I'm really tired of this crap, Hugh."

"Cecil, I can't find 'ix-nay'. How do you spell it?"

"Forget it, Todd. I'll tell you later."

"That's it. That's it." Linda pressed her hands flat against the dash of the car. "I'm sorry, but I can only take so much. You pick up these two men. They are talking in code and reading from . . . some book. I don't care if you want to be Ken Kesey or whatever. I don't have to take these kinds of risks, just to preserve my youth. Pull over. Pull over."

Hugh shrugged, plainly embarrassed, and he signaled and pulled over to the shoulder. We were at least a half mile from the next exit. Linda turned around. "I'm sorry. I'm sure you may be very nice people but you shouldn't be hitchhiking in the first place. It's dangerous and leaves everyone exposed."

"Exposed?" Toddy looked at me, confused.

Linda charged ahead. "I'm sure you can come up with something. Give them some money, Hugh."

"What are you talking about?" He turned to her.

"You heard me, Captain Trips!"

"For gosh sakes." Hugh fished into his pants, brought out a wallet, and handed me a twenty-dollar bill. "Here ya go, fellas. I'm sorry. That's all I have," he said as he tried to hide the other bills in his leather wallet.

I opened the door and stepped out into the sucking noise of the freeway. Toddy jumped out and shut the door.

"They seemed like nice people," he said to me just as a police cruiser pulled up behind us.

The police officer was really very nice. He ran our names and numbers to check for warrants, then gave us a ride to the next exit. He told us to be careful. We were south of downtown Seattle but not around the corner or over the hill to the airport. A fresh breeze riffled our hair and there was a slight mist of rain in the air. We had been traveling an hour and had made about three miles. Toddy held out his thumb.

"You know, Cecil, I was extremely anxious about hitchhiking but I can see that it may be a very fruitful and fecund method to meet extraordinary people."

After an hour a new black Jeep Cherokee with smoked windows pulled up. A young black man in a Chicago Bulls warm-up jacket stepped out. His skin was shiny as coal and he wore a blue bandanna under his ballcap, which was turned backwards.

"Get in," he said, in a way that did not seem like a request.

I grabbed for Todd's sleeve to stop him, but he walked straight toward the Jeep and, smiling at the young man, got right into the car.

"Todd. Todd," I blurted out. "Come on out." But he was already in a conversation with another man in the backseat and the man holding the door waved me in as if he were pleased to be my chauffeur. I slid into the backseat and there was another young black man by the window. The first man got back in so Todd and I were tightly jammed between them. He had a beautiful diamond stud in his ear that reminded me of a winter star. Music was pumping. There were two men in the front. The passenger pointed to the tape player and the driver turned the music off.

"Well, like I said, we're headed to Centralia," Toddy said in a friendly voice. The man in the passenger seat had lighter skin and wore a heavy silver ID chain on one wrist and a dulled gold bracelet as thick as a handcuff on the other. He had hooded, sleepy eyes, the whites of which seemed yellow and bloodshot. He nodded and the Jeep pulled out into traffic.

There was something on the floor of the backseat. It was covered with another jacket. As I started to put my foot down the man on my right touched my knee and politely said, "Be careful, man." I put my feet up on the transmission hump. The man on the left carefully wrapped whatever it was in the jacket and placed it in the back cargo compartment. I could hear a muffled metallic clicking behind me. He said, "It's okay," and that was it.

Toddy looked around at the men in the car and said, "Well, are you guys on a sports team or something?"

The driver turned to the passenger with an angry glance, then he looked at us bunched up in the backseat and he laughed. "Nawwwww!" he drawled, and they all broke into a gentle smoky laugh. "Naw. We're not on a sports team." The driver shook his head sadly as if we must be too stupid to be worth considering.

Todd mentioned again that we were headed to Centralia. The front passenger nodded and smiled easily. He looked back at Todd. "We're just doing a trip. You'll get there."

We pulled off the freeway and went up over the hill and headed to the east. Soon we were driving down a broad avenue with public housing on the right side of the street. I looked at the riders. They were sitting up straighter in their seats. Their bodies were tense. My hands clenched and I felt the prickle of sweat itch my skin. I noticed my breathing was shallow.

The front passenger looked at me. He scowled slightly. "Ain't nothing. Just relax. Sit." He smiled at me and motioned to the man next to me, who reached over and touched my jacket down to my waist. He took my bag and Toddy's dictionary and put them in the back of the Jeep.

We drove down a side street. There was a gas station and a boarded-up house on the north side of the street. There was an abandoned school to the south. As we pulled up, six young black men walked through a tear in the chain-link fencing. Four of them had red warm-up jackets on. Even though it was warm enough they all had their coats buttoned up. One man had a black leather coat and he walked stiff-legged. There was a boy with them who looked to be about twelve years old. He was not wearing a warm-up jacket at all but had a white T-shirt. The older boys were ignoring him and as he walked under the tilted basketball hoop, he jumped for the rim, missing it only by inches. One of the men was a very tall and muscular man who had a splint on two fingers of his right hand. He walked faster than the others. The others hung back and watched our Jeep carefully. The man with the splint came to the driver's side of our Jeep and stood with his feet widely spaced, both hands in his pockets. He stood back about four feet from the car. If the driver of the Jeep had a gun in his lap he was going to have to raise it up at least to window height to get a shot off.

The splint man looked at Todd and me, then said, " 'Sup with the cream, man?"

"Just riding," the front passenger replied in a calm voice that was a little too loud. The man sitting next to me was jouncing his knees up and down. In his lap, his hands were shaking.

The splint man spit on the ground and stepped quickly away from the Jeep. "Mother*fucker!*" he blurted out. He walked back to the other five men who were standing shoulder to shoulder facing the Jeep. They spoke for about thirty seconds. Several seemed to be disagreeing with the splint man. The man in the black coat never spoke and never took his eyes off our car or his hands out of his deep pockets.

Finally the splint man said something to the kid. He ran eagerly back through the torn fence. He was fast and graceful. He reappeared almost instantly with a shiny metal briefcase, the type that photographers transport their expensive cameras in. The front passenger in the Jeep motioned to the man on my right. He instantly jumped out and opened the rear gate. I looked at the open door and for a minute considered the possibility of lunging out, but decided against it. The kid laid the case in the back of the Jeep. The rider slid back in next to me and the splint man came closer.

"*Fuck* you, man."

"Maybe," our front passenger said. Then he waved and the driver turned the Jeep slowly around in the middle of the street. It wasn't until we turned around that I saw the police car parked under the island of the gas station. Two officers were in the car watching us in the playground. One was eating a sandwich. Both were white men.

Everyone was laughing and hooting, slapping five as we roared up over the hill to the freeway. No one said a thing to us until they pulled over at the exact same exit where they had picked us up. They pulled over and opened the door. The front passenger rolled down his window, smiled with an easy drawl, and said, "Get yourself a car, man. Hitchhiking is dangerous shit." He chuckled and the others hooted and laughed. He held up his black fist which was festooned with gold rings. "Peace," he said, and the Jeep lurched away into traffic. Our bag and Toddy's dictionary flew out the back window and rolled on the pavement.

I knelt down on the stubble of grass on the edge of the pavement and vomited for the second time that day. Toddy was peeved. He paced up the road and retrieved our stuff.

"Cecil!" he whined, "they brought us right back here."

"Yeah, I know," I said, and I spit on the grass trying to scrape the sour taste off my tongue.

Toddy walked toward me. "Were they playing a practical joke on us?" he asked. He was already holding his thumb out.

"This is not working, buddy," I said weakly. "This is the nineties. We can't be out here hitchhiking."

Just as those words escaped my lips, a puke-green

Chevy van stopped on the ramp. "Extraordinary," I said, and Todd ran to open the door. But it was locked.

There were three young white people hovering inside looking out the side passenger's window at us. One of them, almost certainly a female, was holding down the button of the door lock.

"We were thinking of giving you guys a ride, you know. But *no* weird stuff. Okay?"

Todd smiled at them, but asked, "Weird stuff? I'm not sure I know what you mean." No, how could he, I thought. After all, we are aliens visiting earth for the first time.

The people in the van laughed and the girl, who I could see now was very pretty, with close-cropped black hair and a hoop pierced through her eyebrow, was waving her palm in front of her face as if she were counteracting our smell.

"You know, no guns or knives and stuff. We are *really* not into weapons."

I held my hands up and turned around. "No guns," I said, and I held my coat open.

"Oh, no," Toddy added quickly. "Cecil doesn't carry a gun. The police won't let him. Ever since he went to jail that time they say he can't ever carry a gun."

Slumping against the van I moaned, "Oh, Christ." All the eyes in the van were on us. One of the passengers got back behind the driver's seat, pulling on the gearshift.

"Listen," I pleaded, "we just want to get to Centralia." I held my hands up to the windows. "I promise you we're okay. I mean, we're . . . eccentric, but essentially nonviolent."

"You were in jail?" the girl yelled through the glass. Her pretty brown eyes were wide and showed more fascination than fear. I have to admit I had to force myself not to stare at her pierced eyebrow.

"For suborning perjury," I yelled, as if I were talking to a foreigner or someone hard of hearing. "They said I caused someone to lie under oath. It's a nonviolent offense."

"What about the drugs?" Toddy spoke up to be helpful. I almost started to cry.

"I'm getting to that, all right?" I snapped at him. "Possession of cocaine. All right. I was set up. They videotaped me snorting a line of cocaine. I know I shouldn't have done it, and I have completely rehabilitated myself. Okay? That's it. I forged my parents' name on a report card, but I don't think my educational records are germane to my qualifications to ride in your van."

"Are you guys gay?" the girl said doubtfully.

This must be how people are forced into a life of crime. I would much rather have car-jacked the van than keep up this audition on the on-ramp.

"What would make you feel better about us?" I asked her.

The girl bit the end of her finger and screwed her face up into a grimace of thought. "I suppose I'd feel better if you were gay," she finally offered.

"Geez, Connie, let's go," the male voice behind the wheel implored. I put my hand on the glass of the window, close to Connie's face.

"Well, we're not gay. But I promise if you can get us any closer to Centralia, the subject of sex will *not* come up."

"Connniieeee!" the voice whined.

"Fuck it," she said and flipped open the door lock.

As we entered the van, Toddy spoke to me earnestly. "I don't think you need to mention your driving violations, Cecil, seeing as how you won't be driving their van."

"Yeah, thanks," I muttered and flopped down on the mattress that was set up in the back bed.

The Grateful Dead were playing from the tape deck.

The quality of the tape was poor and there was quite a bit of crowd sound in the foreground so I took it for a boot-legged recording of a concert. There were beaded shades on the side windows that tapped against the glass as the van accelerated into the middle lane. A tie-dyed quilt covered the old mattress. The two boys shared the driving and navigating in the front as Connie sat cross-legged and leaned against the locked door. Todd sat on the mattress and looked carefully at his dictionary, picking at the small cuts on the cover.

I looked behind and there were bales of tie-dyed clothes: reds and blue-greens that were only found in the early years of color television.

"I saw The Dead in concert once," I offered lamely. "In Iowa City."

Silence. Connie smiled vaguely. Bored, as if by her late teens she had already grown weary of old people attempting to relate to her. She rolled her head languidly. "It's not like we're Deadheads or anything." She puffed her breath over her upper lip as if she were blowing her bangs off her forehead. Only she didn't have bangs anymore. "I mean, for gosh sakes. Jerry's dead. It's all so archaic."

"Yeah, I know," I said, not knowing what else to say. I closed my eyes as the van bumped on the concrete and the music galloped like a pony.

But Connie didn't want to be ignored. Apparently we were in her charge as the boys weren't going to have anything to do with us.

"We're just going down to Olympia. There's an Irish music festival out near the Trident submarine base. We're going to sell tie-dye there. It's so lame." Connie rolled her eyes, and gestured with her chin in the general direction of the entire lame world.

"I mean, all these people. They are all used up. You know, just trying to reclaim the sixties or something. I don't know," she shrugged. "But it's pretty good money for the three of us."

"What are you going to do with the money?" I asked.

"Well, Mike—" she gestured with her head to the driver, "he wants to go to boat-building school in Maine, and Jonathan—" here she pointed and I noticed her fingers were exceptionally fine and white, "Jonathan's putting money into his music."

"How about you? What are you saving for?"

She smiled and her weariness dropped away suddenly. She was so lovely, even with the shorn hair and pierced body parts. I turned away from her, afraid I was going to release some "lecher energy." She bent over and touched my knee.

"I've got land payments," she whispered and shrugged her shoulders like a happy child.

"What kind of land?" I asked the traffic past the window.

"It's just a little tiny lot on the ocean, over in Moclips. It's got a few trees and some grass and stuff. The trailer is nothing, really. But it's dry and it doesn't smell, you know, like how old trailers smell?"

I nodded, knowing exactly what she meant.

Connie rolled over on her knees and moved in to lean against the wall of the van near us. Toddy stared unashamedly at the ring cutting through her eyebrow.

"It's perfect," Connie continued. "It's on a one-lane sand road at the foot of a hill. When you look out from my lot, the trees look like one of those Japanese screens, you know? The trees are all bent over and gnarled in the direction of the wind. The grass blows around, all green and yellow." Connie's eyes were closed and her hands were spread in front of her as if she were laying it out for us.

"Then, past the trees it's flat sand. Huge. People

drive on it. But not too much, you know, 'cause there aren't that many people around. The sand is flat and the breakers churn all the time. Churn all the time, so it's never really quiet." She drew her hand out as if she were stringing a long thread.

"It's not like the mountains. I like the mountains, but this is different. The beach, and the ocean is so huge when you look out it's restful. It's so . . . horizontal."

For a few moments she didn't speak and the rush of the traffic could have been ocean breakers.

"Pheww!" She blew her imaginary bangs off her forehead again and opened her eyes. "That must sound like real hippie shit."

"It sounds nice," I offered, instead of an intelligent comment.

"Well, my parents are Republican golf addicts. What about your parents?"

We rode for fifty miles talking about our parents. Mike and Jonathan joined in, mostly in agreement on the final hopelessness of ever fully understanding anything substantial. I told them how my father had died at the foot of a slot machine after winning a hundred-thousand-dollar jackpot, and I thought Connie was going to wet herself laughing so hard. Then she pulled back and collected herself, trying to look sad, but only succeeded in looking embarrassed. "But that's terrible," she said, stifling her laughter.

Toddy told all about his mother and only mentioned his father in passing. He told Connie about his mother's sweet disposition. He described what she wore, how she smiled and how she had been able to talk to him even after she had died. Connie, Mike, and Jonathan listened and nodded, never betraying the slightest judgment or skepticism. Mike told how he wanted eventually to build a sailboat that could be fitted for salmon trolling, and I gave him the name of a rigger in Anacortes that I had met on one of my old drug cases. I told Mike that this rigger would like his idea and might have some gear for him when he was ready.

Finally we approached the off-ramp they were going to take just south of the capitol building in Olympia. We exchanged addresses, and Connie insisted on giving us both tie-dyed T-shirts. Todd put his on over his cardigan sweater.

I stuffed my T-shirt into the top of Todd's bag as I got out of the van across from the on-ramp. Connie kissed Toddy and told him to take good care of himself. She moved in toward me for a kiss, then pulled away instead and shook my hand with both of hers. She looked at me warily but smiled and rubbed the back of my hand with her thumb. "This should be a good ramp for you guys. Lots of college kids. Lots of traffic south toward Portland and stuff." She dropped my hand. "Come to the ocean sometime."

"I'd like to," I told her. She got back into the van and they pulled away.

The on-ramp was closer to the trees than anything we had seen in Seattle. The sun was lower in the sky and the shadows were long. I looked at Toddy, with his bristly short hair, his fluorescent tie-dyed T-shirt stretched tight over the weird bulges of his other clothes. He was clutching his dictionary like an IRA bomber walking into Harrods. I sighed and thought the Oregon Trail must be shorter than this route to Centralia. Then I stuck out my thumb, closed my eyes, and tried to re-create the sound of the freeway as surf breaking. Trucks blared and the thumping of powerful stereo systems swelled in the Doppler rush, causing me to open my eyes again. There were some birds in the trees but I couldn't hear them and I couldn't recognize their shapes. We watched a yellow cat successfully dart and dodge across the eight lanes of traffic. Some cars slowed and others honked. Toddy and I cheered as the cat sprang up a Douglas fir tree on the far side of the road.

Finally an old Mazda hatchback pulled over. It was

belching smoke from the exhaust and it appeared to have been painted with green house paint. It stopped fifty yards past us and the driver looked back and opened the passenger door. Toddy got into the backseat and I settled into the front.

The driver had shoulder-length gray hair. He wore a black cowboy shirt and he had a video recorder and a .44 Magnum on his lap. He was rocking back and forth on his seat gripping the steering wheel so hard that his knuckles were white.

He told us he was an artist and that he would give us a ride to the outlet stores outside of Centralia if he could interview us. I told him he had to put the gun away and he slid it between his cowboy boots and under his seat as he pulled into the southbound traffic.

It was a strange interview. The artist didn't ask any questions because he was too busy telling us what he thought of this impoverished and insincere world.

"Authenticity. That's what my work's about. That's why I picked you guys up. I'm going to chronicle the last authentic experiences a person can have in this plastic-wrapped, postmodern shitbag of a western world." He said the word "postmodern" with more distaste than when he said the word "shitbag."

"Uh-huh," I said as neutrally as I could manage, not knowing which direction this interview was going or how I was expected to weigh in on the topic of "authenticity."

"So . . ." I offered tentatively, "what makes an experience authentic?"

"They jump up straight out of the ground like dead animals come back to life," he blurted out in a weird croak, his hands tight on the steering wheel.

He straightened up and stretched the small of his back, shaking his head back and forth, never taking his eyes off the road. He was silent for a time as if he were going into a trance, and he may have been, for all I knew, because when he spoke his voice seemed deep and urgent.

"You read Stephen King?" He was looking at me now. His eyes could have had yellow slit irises but I may not be remembering that correctly. I nodded that I had read King, thinking I surely must have.

"Then you know what I mean. The man's a fucking genius."

"No argument there," I chirped breezily, looking back at Todd who was happily watching the river of cars on the freeway. I checked my door, making sure it was unlocked.

"Horror," the artist said, and then he said nothing more for a minute. A tractor trailer with a load of wallboard was adjusting its straps on the side of the road. A highway patrol car was stopped behind. A middle-aged man in a BMW drove slowly past us on the right. He was talking on a cellular phone. Cigarette smoke circled his head lazily. Toddy waved at him and he sped away from us.

"Horror is the one thing left that will define the authentic." Our host changed lanes and sped up to follow the BMW. "Death has become cheapened, overused, numbed. And love? Shit! Forget it. Country western songs . . . ads for expensive cars . . ."

He sped up until the bumper of his car was several feet from the BMW's. His index finger was ticking the wheel as he continued to stare ahead.

"What do you take seriously? What do you absolutely believe without question or argument? Horror's it. The baseline, the place we all start from. We all bullshit ourselves about love and death and loyalty and money and sex and sex and sex. But horror . . . the bare wire in the bottom of our brain where all the fires start: razors and split eyes."

He was smiling at me now, the veins on the side of his neck distended. His face was growing red. I was easing into the door to position myself so that if he reached for the gun under his seat I could lift my foot over the hump of the transmission and kick his hand, then perhaps pull up on the hand brake. I was squirming under the seat belt shoulder strap when he lifted up the camera in one hand and pointed it in my face.

In a low voice the driver said, "Tell me what you're most afraid of." I could see the green light on the front of the camera blinking.

Toddy leaned forward and put his huge bristly head between the seats. He leaned so close to the camera that the driver had to hold it back near the corner of the windshield.

"Frankly, I'm afraid that Jane Marie is angry with my dog, Wendall," Toddy said. "He's just a young dog, you know, and he sometimes chews on rather expensive shoes. Cecil often gets extremely agitated with him, but I have to point out that Wendall is only responding to instinct. Instinct is a very powerful urge, don't you think?"

"Instinct for what?" the driver asked, frowning, not liking the way this interview was going.

"Well," Toddy drawled out. "I suppose I was referring to the instinct to chew shoes."

I started to laugh and the driver plopped his camera into his lap and angrily flicked on his turn signal.

I was still laughing as we were walking up the exit. The driver had opened my door, shoved a piece of paper into my hand, and pointed to the open door. Toddy and I hopped out into the late afternoon light that was bathing the convenience store and truck stop in a holy light. At the top of the exit I could see the row of outlet stores built on the flat river bottom that identified the exit for the towns of Centralia and Chehalis. Their lights rose softly into the sky. Just beyond the signs I could make out a green iron bridge across a slow-moving river.

I looked at the piece of paper. It turned out to be an

unsigned release. It read: *You have just taken part in a guer-rilla film called "The Faces of Fear" by veteran underground film maker Edward Alex. Please sign this release form and send it to the address marked on the back. If you do, you will be entitled to a share of the profits from the production. Your share will be determined by your cooperation and participation in the film. "Dead Right Productions" retains all rights and considerations of the materials gathered.*

I crumpled up the paper and stuck it down Todd's pack. In the distance I could hear a train whistle. I was suddenly very happy.

I have seen awful things in my life. I watched the death of my father and held the limp body of a child who had blown his own arm off. Just this afternoon I had been splashed with a strange woman's urine and had vomited twice in public, so it was too late to think of myself as Pollyanna. But walking uphill with Todd, I was beginning to feel optimistic and almost clean. I was thinking that although this world can be uncommonly cruel and horror is doled out capriciously, I didn't think there is anything more powerful than this ordinary and complex humanness.

"You know, you are a good guy to travel with," I told Todd as we walked down the narrow road that led to town.

Toddy looked at me with his puzzled and comical expression. "Thank you, Cecil." He walked on in silence for a few steps looking down at the gravel on the side of the road.

Then he blurted out, "I suppose you are, too. But I really don't have a broad base of experience from which to judge."

A truck with tree planters picked us up and we rode in the back bed. No one in the truck spoke English but it was made plain they were headed into town to meet some friends. There were canvas bags for the seedlings and short-handled picks with flat digging blades piled by the rear gate. A young boy had unwrapped his dinner from a roll of newspaper on his lap. He motioned Todd to hand him the dictionary and thinking that he wanted to look something up, Todd handed it over. The boy set the dictionary on his lap and used it as a table. He set a flour tortilla filled with beans on the cover, using his pocket knife to cut the tortilla in half, then one half into quarters. He handed a quarter slice to both Toddy and me. The beans burned slow with peppers. Toddy's eyes started to tear as he chewed and the men in the truck laughed. Someone offered water and they patted Todd on the back and talked about buying beer in town.

The road was narrow, with small residential houses set back from it. There were a few old willows in the yards, fir trees rising out of the muddy grass. Darkness was coming on and across the flat river bottom I could see a dairy barn and a thin layer of fog clinging to a pasture where black-and-white cows stood quietly, only occasionally twitching their tails.

Finally the street widened into a straight boulevard lined with shop fronts and gas stations. The buildings had high square fronts above their peaked roofs. More and more of them were red brick with old-fashioned plate glass fronts. At a stoplight in what was beginning to look like the oldest part of the town, the streets were cobblestone for a short stretch. There was a Hispanic social club on one corner. Several men who were standing on the corner near the social club waved and walked over to the truck. Todd and I clambered out, and as the truck drove away the young boy stood up suddenly and banged on the roof, yelling to the driver. The truck braked midintersection and the boy jumped from the bed and ran across the cobblestones to us carrying the dictionary Todd had left behind. He darted back as the truck was moving down the street and the older men hauled him back onto the bed by grabbing him by the belt, pulling him on.

Todd stood waving to the truck. Up the first side street I saw the Centralia American Legion Hall, Post Number 17, and past that was a brick building with a little park beyond it and a statue of a doughboy standing sentinel. Todd and I walked into the park and I tried to look both ways down the streets to see if there was a phone booth anywhere near. I was hoping for something like a phone book with a street address and a map. Todd went to look at the statue.

No luck with the phone booth. As I walked up behind Todd, I heard him murmuring the words he was reading.

" 'We live in deeds, not years, in thoughts, not breaths, in feelings, not figures on a dial.' " Todd was dwarfed by the bronze statue on its marble slab: a World War I soldier holding his rifle at ease, with his long coat buttoned and his collar up. Toddy kept murmuring, "Arthur McElfresh and Warren Grimm."

"What did you say, Todd?"

"It's his name, Cecil. I just said his name. It's Warren Grimm. I wasn't saying a word or anything. It's his name, like I told you."

I walked around the side where Todd was reading and looked at the names of the soldiers, then moved quickly around to the other side and read: *To the memory of Ben Casagranda, Warren O. Grimm, Ernest Dale Hubbard, Arthur McElfresh. Slain on the streets of Centralia, Washington, Armistice Day Nov. 11, 1919 while on peaceful parade wearing the uniform of the country they loyally and faithfully served.*

"We're in the right town, anyhow." I was talking to myself. Toddy looked up at me quizzically.

"Can we go home now?" he asked with a tone of hope rising in his voice.

"No," I told him. "I'm looking for a man who knows about Warren Grimm and how he died."

"How are we going to find the man you are looking for, Cecil?" Todd stood flat-footed, his shoulders drooping.

He squinted at me through the thick lenses of his broken glasses.

"We need to find a bar," I offered weakly.

Todd looked at me skeptically. "Are you sure the man you are looking for will be there?" he asked as I turned away from the statue and him and started walking.

"No." I said it to my shoes.

"Are you sure the man you're looking for is even in this town?" Todd's voice was catching up to me as I quickened my pace back toward the old main street.

"No," I said again.

"Couldn't we have telephoned ahead to make sure?" Todd was walking next to me now.

"We need to surprise him, Todd," I said stiffly.

Todd pushed his glasses up his nose and tried to walk backward in front of me so that he could look me in the eye.

"It won't be much of a surprise if he isn't here, will it, Cecil?" he asked me with an irritatingly naive tone.

"No. It won't" was all I could offer.

Chapter Eight

I ran into Marcus by the edge of the bar. Toddy bumped into my back and we jostled to a stop like a blind pack train. "Jesus, you made it here in a hurry," Marcus said, eyeing me warily.

"Where is Simon Delaney, and where's the money? Answer the second part first," I said into the buttons of Marcus's white shirt.

"The money is safe," Marcus said into the mouth of his coffee cup. "Simon is in the back. Don't harass him. He's not doing very well." Marcus drained the white coffee mug, slammed it down on the mahogany bar, and moved past us and toward the door. Then he turned around. "Did you bring my coat?" he asked.

"No, I didn't bring your coat," I said, trying not to sound too peeved at the massive man across from me.

"I gotta go." Marcus nodded, turned, then was out the door.

Marcus was so large that when he left it felt like someone had felled a huge tree, leaving Toddy and me in a clearing. That feeling was short-lived however, because the next swing of the door brought in a beefy white boy made tall by new-looking cowboy boots.

According to the plaque near the beer sign, the poolroom had been built in 1889, and it looked as if it had never been remodeled. From the street, a heavy wooden awning hung over the sidewalk. Under the awning was a dusty candy stand with curved glass cases. The doors of the poolroom were dark heavy wood with etched glass and brass hardware. Next to the bar was a steamy lunchroom with rickety wooden chairs bolted around a counter. The dusty sign indicated it was under new management. The hand-painted sign read TORTILLARÍA. I could smell cornmeal and beer as Todd and I walked toward the poolroom, both of us squinting and gawking at the Tiffany chandeliers with tulip patterns. To the left of the bar was a coal furnace partitioning off a card room and past that were the pool tables with the old leather webbing. The floor was cracked concrete. Shreds of several generations of flooring showed through the corners.

The scoring beads hung limply on sagging wires. The suspended ceiling was yellowed and falling down. Every surface in the room was covered with a fine layer of dust. The shaded lights above each table cast harsh and slanted shadows onto the faces of the players who moved like workmen with their cues around the tables.

In the corner, slumped into one of the raised wooden seats, sat a man with raven hair and a wobbly stare.

"I know you from Sitka. You're the dick. Right?" Simon Delaney slurred.

A coffee-can spittoon teetered on the chair next to him. I moved it to the floor and stepped up to sit in the old wood theater seat, which rested a little lower than shoeshine height against the back wall. Toddy lumbered into his seat still clutching his bag and his dictionary. We looked like refugees from a garage sale.

"Christ, you stink!" Simon Delaney bellowed, but only one player looked up from his shot. I sniffed the sleeve of my wool coat and confirmed that my jacket still smelled like piss from the bus station a world away.

"Yeah, I know," I said cleverly.

Simon Delaney's eyes glittered and his torso swayed even as he sat still. He was smoking a cigarette loosely held between his fingertips. He held the cigarette like a kid learning to smoke. He puffed it through pursed lips, squinting into the smoke.

"You here about Angela?" He lurched forward, expelling smoke through a broken tooth. When he did, he almost toppled off the chair and I propped him back in his seat.

"Yeah, I'd like to talk about Angela with you . . . sometime." I tried to hand him his drink from the floor between his legs.

"Noooo. Ass. Hole." Simon Delaney sputtered, then made a fist with his right hand. "Did . . . you . . . hear . . . about Angela?" He held his fist up in front of me. "She's dead." He said it with startling clarity, tears welling up in his eyes.

"I know." I nodded and continued to hold his highball glass, which I guessed was vodka and Coke. "How'd that happen?"

He waved me off and knocked the drink out of my hand. The glass shattered. Ice cubes scattered on the concrete floor. The nearest pool player glanced only once at us as the heel of his workboot ground a shard of glass into the concrete.

"Don't worry. I'm a drunk. I hope Marcus told you that. I'm a drunk. My father was a drunk Irishman. So I'm good at it. You know?" He glared at me, wanting an answer. I knew enough to wait. This wasn't a conversation, not with me at least. Simon Delaney was talking to a chorus of old and neglected demons.

"My mom was Chinese and Swedish. She worked in this bar. You know. The dark side always gets noticed in a town like this. She was a Chink to everyone." He stared at me, letting the words float to the bottom of the glass. I stayed still. "Anyway, she got knocked up by Angus Delaney. He said he was a gunman." He waved his hand at an imaginary fly. "A gunman for Christsakes in the Irish Republican Army." Simon touched the side of his nose as if it were a magical gesture. "Bastard never was no gunman. He was a drunk. Never did a goddamn thing. We lived in Ireland for a little while. Worked in a tractor factory, then came back here to work in this bar." Simon raised his hands to the dilapidated pool hall, smiling like an imp. "What's that tell you about his commitment to the revolution?" Here Simon tried to erase the memory with his hands. "This political shit doesn't mean anything, anyway," he blurted.

An older man with a dark, weathered face entered the poolroom. He wore a straw work hat and a cheap windbreaker over his work coveralls. He was with a young man who could have been his son. They looked around, then walked to the far corner of the room near where a beefy white kid was playing the table by himself, watched by his blond girlfriend.

"Marcus and his workers. There are no fucking workers. There are just assholes. Assholes and people without jobs who ASS PIRE to be assholes."

The older man was inquiring about his turn at the pool table. He spoke broken English with a heavy Spanish accent. He pointed to the quarter on the table where he had set it. The beefy white boy in the T-shirt and cowboy boots ignored him. He racked the balls again. The old man spoke something in Spanish and the white kid ignored him.

"Marcus and his bullshit revolution . . . Check this

out," Simon Delaney muttered. He pulled himself to his feet, rocking unsteadily, his smile screwed into a mocking leer. "Comrades!" he called out. Three of the men around the tables looked up, maybe bemused, maybe angry. "Comrades! You create the wealth that is denied you! You are slaves to people who hate you. Who hate your children. Yet you thank them with your loyalty—."

"Shut the Chink up," I heard a player say back in the gloom.

"Buy him a drink," said another.

Simon slumped down in the seat. The pool balls clattered and someone put money in the jukebox.

"You know, dick . . ." Simon Delaney turned to me. "This revolution . . . this communalism or whatever the fuck it was . . . was really only supposed to be . . . was only supposed to be . . . a kind of generosity. A goodness of heart."

A country western song came wheezing and yodeling out of the jukebox. Simon looked around the poolroom. "Generosity. Shit. These bastards deserve everything they get." Delaney spat out the words. He threw his cigarette into the coffee can.

"Fuckit . . ." he muttered.

In the corner, the white kid was talking loud about "trained monkeys" and "field niggers." His blond girlfriend sat in one of the rickety wooden seats along the back wall. She laughed nervously but didn't take her eyes off the boy. Todd stood and went to the far corner to play some pinball. The two Mexican men were sitting quietly drinking their beer and the redneck boy was trying trick shots to amuse his girlfriend. Simon turned back to me.

"Angela was a smart woman, you know. She was smart enough to know that she was getting screwed over. She hated it in that little trailer. She wanted a real place. She wanted a goat and shit. Christ! Mexicans think having a goat makes 'em rich. You know?"

The pretty white boy was taking his time doing trick shots and ignoring the two Mexican men waiting with their quarter on the table. They walked over and spoke affably to Toddy who was worrying the sides of the pinball machine, his face contorted into a mask of concentration. The boy who was doing the pool tricks scowled. In a loud voice he asked his girlfriend if it didn't smell like beans in the bar. The girlfriend giggled, but her skin was growing red and she started to shred the wrapper off her beer bottle nervously.

"I know you were there when she died." I tried to keep my voice to a monotone, hoping to stay out of Simon's conversation with the booze. "How'd it happen?"

"She was going crazy, man." Simon was sinking back into himself, disappearing. "She'd been drinking for days. I split on the ferry but came back on a friend's fishing boat. I couldn't leave those two kids. I mean, she was going crazy. She'd been in that trailer all winter. She didn't have any friends in that fucking town. She was drinking and saying she was going to kill herself. She said she was proud. Too proud for welfare, you know? She gets that from her father. Poor and proud . . . all that immigrant shit."

The Mexican man racked up the balls. He and his son were going to get a table. The pretty white boy left his table and brought his cue toward our end of the room. He was standing next to the line of chairs where we were sitting. He was trying to get the attention of the older man lining up to take his shot. The old man winked at me and then quickly sighted his cue and shot the ball, knocking a striped one into the corner. "Big ones," he said to his son in English. Todd was watching their game now. Smiling with them. The white boy was breathing harder and pressing his arms against his chest as he leaned against his cue. The effect gave the impression that his biceps were more muscled than they were. I kept looking at Todd, wanting to get him out of there.

"She had a gun. It was self-defense . . ." Simon

reached over and touched my elbow. Slowly and clearly he said, "All the killing in the world is done in self-defense. Didn't you know that?"

The pretty white boy was pulling away from his girlfriend. He was still talking loudly about getting trained monkeys to pick fruit. His girl clung to him and he made a show of pulling away from her and then he would move in for a sloppy tongue kiss before he continued threatening the two men in the corner.

"Hey, monkey-boy, you speak English? What the fuck you doing looking at my girl?" The pretty boy was bulging his chest as best he could and he had a two-fisted grip on the midsection of his cue. The old man looked up from the table and said softly, *"Bonita,"* and then made his shot.

"So you saw old Flynn shoot Angela in self-defense?" I asked, not taking my eyes off the scene. Simon Delaney followed my eyes and we both stood up. Then he looked at me, puzzled.

"Is that what you think?" he asked and he stood still, taking in a deep breath and seeming more stable on his feet. Then he released his breath slowly. Looking at me all the while.

A glass broke and the pretty boy was shaking in rage. He was looking down at his feet and there were shards of broken glass and spilled beer there. The young Mexican player had spilled a glass near the pretty boy when he was making his last shot.

"These are handmade boots, motherfucker."

The young man reached into his pocket and the old man looked at the boots and said, *"Lo siento,"* very softly and then took his son by the elbow and walked slowly away from the table.

"Get back here, monkey!" the pretty boy called.

I started walking toward Todd. "Let's get out of here, buddy," I called out to him.

The pretty boy spun on his heel. "What you say?" He glared at me. "What you say to me?" he hissed. His girl-friend had her head buried in her hands, her pretty blond hair hanging down to her elbows. It shook like laundry on the line from her sobbing.

Simon Delaney walked calmly to the rack of sticks and broke down a two-piece cue. The pretty white boy was quivering like a racehorse, his fists clenched, and he stood on the balls of his feet leaning forward. Toward me.

I held my palms up. I shook my head and took a step back, and as I did Simon Delaney slammed the boy's face with the fat end of the pool cue.

The crack sounded like a breaking rock. Blood sprayed up onto the lights. The boy's head fell hard on the edge of the pool table, spraying more blood on the green felt and in the dust on the concrete. Toddy was shrinking back into the corner. At first men moved away from the bloody boy and Simon Delaney, who was standing over him. Shadows from the swinging light lurched around the room. Then men moved forward.

I tried to get to Todd but was blocked by three men in brown coveralls holding pool cues. It dawned on me then: These guys were thinking Simon and I had worked the sucker punch together. I pushed away from a canvas jacket. I bit someone's fingers and ran toward the back door just behind Simon Delaney.

The voices died away after three blocks. The evening air was moist but warmer somehow than I was used to in Alaska. We could hear a train rumble in the yard a block away. But no sirens. We slowed to a walk. Simon Delaney had a stiff-legged cowboy walk with a gimp and a two-beat cadence to his footfall. Heel, toe, heel, toe, slapping the side-walk. I bunched my hands in my pockets. I stopped suddenly, feeling light without my pack. Without Todd. I started to double back for Todd but Delaney grabbed me.

"Bullshit, man. You don't know these guys. There will be no talking if you go back that way."

I nodded and stepped down off the curb at the end of the block. We were walking quickly out of the downtown area. I would give the bar a few minutes to cool off, then I'd walk back and gather up Todd.

The streets were opening up to the sky. We walked in silence. Maybe it was the night air or it could have been the violence but something had caused Simon Delaney to sober up somewhat, though he still careened from one edge of the sidewalk to the other. Finally, we stopped on Fourth and Trower, across the street from a crumbling concrete facade. Simon Delaney pointed to a low wooded hill that I could see only dimly across the railroad yards.

"That's Seminary Hill. Armistice Day, 1919: Three shooters were there. They carried two of the guns and all their ammunition in an old suitcase. They took a position under the water tower and then moved down as the parade came close. Loren Roberts, Burt Bland, and of course . . . Ole Hanson." He turned and pointed up and down the street.

"Hotels are gone. The hall is gone." Simon walked out into the middle of the deserted street. The clerk at the convenience store across the street looked out from over his hot dog carousel, shading his eyes to see through the glare on the glass.

"The Legion boys say Warren Grimm was standing right here, right in the middle of this street, when he was shot down like a dog." Simon's oratory was building. His jaw was set and he strode over to the crumbling facade. "That's bullshit. He was a fucking thug, right there, attacking the hall." Simon pounded on the concrete where the plate glass of the old Industrial Workers of the World Hall had once been smashed into a thousand pieces. A truckload of kids drove by, hooting and laughing to the subsonic thump of some huge speakers. One threw a bottle onto the curb near our feet. Simon barely noticed.

"The soldiers were nothing more than a bunch of damn thugs. They were going to destroy the private property of a legitimate political organization. They were a fucking mob. If they were attacking the home of the local doctors and lawyers they would have all been shot without so much as a fucking peep." He hung his head and shoved a glass shard with the toe of his boot.

"There is no peace between the classes," I said, still looking up and down the street, listening for the sirens.

"Right, wiseass. There's no revolution—" The truck full of kids rolled past again, and again they threw a bottle and this time it hit the wall twenty feet to the south of where we stood. Simon Delaney did not flinch.

"You shouldn't have cracked that kid with the cue," I offered as a friendly observation.

Simon Delaney wobbled on his feet and he stared at me as if I were sputum on his boot. "I just saved your ass!" He spit on the ground and kept staring at me. "You are one irritating coward, aren't you?" he snarled.

I shrugged my shoulders, willing to concede the point.

Simon shoved me like an angry child. Then suddenly he hit me hard in the chest and forced me down the alley. I stumbled, looked around for any possible help. "What you going to do about it, nancy boy? You want to be nonviolent, then you want more and more cops to keep your pussy ass protected from the riffraff," Simon Delaney hissed between clenched teeth.

"I'll take you to the old man. I'll take you to Ole Hanson. That's what you're looking for, isn't it? That old man doesn't give a fuck about me or Angela. He just wants Ole." Simon Delaney reached down and grabbed a rock, then threw it so it hit me squarely in the chest. I turned and jogged down the alley, away from his angry voice. Dogs barked behind closed doors. Lights came on. "Run. Come on, run." Simon Delaney was shrieking, throwing muddy stones. We ran hard past several street crossings. I could hear his splashing footfall close behind me.

"What are you going to do? Reason with me?" I could almost feel Simon's words on my back.

I looked around. Simon was a spidery form against the streetlight. He was picking up another rock.

I heard his voice, slurred and puffing but coming on. "At least Wesley had a gun. He shot and ran. Hid, until the bastards came on him, then he shot again. What are *you* going to do?"

We ran up the muddy alley, past a garbage can and a gutted Chevy van. We broke across a main road and up a grassy slope near a storage yard. On the ridge of a hill I stumbled and fell into a thick net of blackberry brambles. It felt like leafy barbed wire. Beneath me the river hissed. I could hear the rounded chuckle of water moving. I lay still, my chest heaving.

If I moved, I felt my weight shift down the slope. If I lay still, I was held by the webbing of thorns. Simon Delaney stood above me, gulping his breaths.

"This is where they caught him. He clawed his way to the river, slowed down by the brambles, he waded out into the current. Wesley knew they were going to kill him. He shot the first one to lunge at him. Killed him on the spot. You could kill me right now, white boy. You know you could and you'd get away with it. But not Wesley. By midnight Wesley was dead and the worst part of it . . ." Simon Delaney held out his hand and helped me disentangle myself from the bramble. My palms and face were bleeding as Simon pulled me to my feet. "The worst part of it was they believed that fucking lawyer when he told them they had the *right* to self-defense."

Simon Delaney had a round river stone in his hand.

"But listen." He raised the stone above me. "The right of self-defense *never* matters to the fucking losers." And he swung the stone down, hitting me at the base of the skull, turning the night into a sparkly haze for an instant, then to nothingness.

Chapter Nine

I woke up in a field that had once been a drive-in movie. My coat and pant legs were covered in dew. The sunlight overhead was an almost sickly yellow. I looked down the length of my body as if it were a ridge line in the Smoky Mountains. At the end of my legs were the pillars of my brown shoes textured with diamonds of moisture.

I heard crows. At least I thought they were crows. And traffic. An empty movie screen rose above me, and on this gray morning the screen seemed more immense than the sky. It was stained with mildew on the seams and some of the screen was peeling. I stared at it for many moments waiting for something to appear. But nothing did. Underneath the screen was a swing set, the rusty chains absolutely still. There was a broken teeter-totter, the light end twisted toward the ground, the heavy end overgrown in grass so the handle was a web of interlacing blades. A truck track matted the grass a few yards away from my legs. The truck had backed around, headlights facing my prone body. It had eased forward, then turned toward the broken gate near the ticket booth where the "No Trespassing" sign swung cockeyed by one wire.

For some reason I kept looking at the swing set, thinking how much I hate them. I see swing sets everywhere I go, out behind little white houses and in the middle of trailer parks. I never see children swinging on them, and the seats are always empty, but even if I'm drunk or riding in a semi truck with the country western music blaring, I can hear the shrieking of their nasty chains, back and forth, back and forth. I was sprawled on the ground in this deserted drive-in movie with a dull-saw-through-the-skull kind of headache, thinking that when people's kids leave home, the government should require them to remove the goddamn swing sets.

I made it to my knees and steadied myself on a crooked speaker post. All of the posts were tilted off of square, the fog had settled just above the cottonwood trees, and a light drizzle was falling silently on the long grass. In the distance a few black-and-white milk cows grazed on the floodplain. My head throbbed to near blindness as I stood up, and I worried about where Todd was and what he must be thinking. Disgusted with the swing set, my eyes searched that huge screen.

I think everybody wishes their life were a movie: the colors more true, the resolution more certain. I rubbed the back of my neck and leaned unsteadily against the speaker post. In my movie I am a dispossessed aristocrat living in a tepee on a sheltered ridge running down to a river valley. Herds of antelope move under the sheltering trees in the distance and a beautiful Indian girl loves me with urgency and conviction. She brings me berries and I bring her meat. We move camp often because our families don't approve of our love. A raven flew out of the fog from the cottonwoods, landing on top of the empty screen, and started heckling me and I knew, finally, that none of that shit was happening. It was all a movie, a bad movie at that, and I had no choice but to go find Toddy and get William Flynn's money back.

I walked out the rutted lane in the overgrown grass

past the old ticket kiosk. I was looking at my shoes as I walked, wondering how far I could walk with wet socks before I would start to raise blisters. I heard a car door open and looked up.

David Ramirez stood on the driver's side by a brand-new Chevrolet Suburban. His blue work shirt was rolled up over his forearms. He wore a gold watch. The passenger side door was open and Ramirez gestured with his thick arm across the hood.

"You look terrible," he said. "Get in."

"I smell like urine," I mentioned.

"I thought you might," he said. "That's why I brought my big car."

The inside of the car smelled new: plastic and clean rubber. David Ramirez turned over the engine and the heater breathed hot dry air. The radio sputtered and he quickly turned it off as he backed around to leave.

"I heard there was some kind of trouble in town last night. I looked all over for you but . . . you must have been hiding out here, huh?" he said as he looked over his shoulder backing up.

"I wouldn't really call it hiding out. More like kidnapped."

"Where is Simon Delaney?" Mr. Ramirez asked flatly, showing no sign of humor or sympathy for my condition.

We pulled out onto a one-way thoroughfare flanked by parking lots and squat buildings: fast food, pavement, square stucco-sided malls with unlit signs showing water stains on the lower edges. A logging truck passed, throwing gravel in a light spray from its rear tires.

"Where are *we*?" I asked finally, ignoring his question.

David Ramirez squinted at the road and said nothing.

"Mr. Ramirez, I don't know where Simon Delaney is right now. I don't know where to find him, but maybe if you told me where we are I could make some kind of start on locating him. Once I get my money back and ask him a few questions you can have him. I absolutely do not care what your business is with him."

Ramirez burned his vision into the windshield. "You two are working together," he hissed.

"All right. Yeah—" I twisted toward him in my seat and started speaking calmly, but felt my voice becoming shrill. "Look, I'm covered in smelly wool, lying out in the rain with my skull bashed in. Which is more likely: That I'm a hopeless fuck-up bumbling around with about half the facts, or that I'm some kind of super secret agent lying out in a deserted drive-in movie waiting to spring a trap on you?"

I reached behind my head and felt the base of my skull. It was meant to be a dramatic gesture, some impromptu gimmick to pull sympathy out of Ramirez, but I was alarmed to find my scalp sticky. My hand was shiny red and I could smell the blood like a tide flat inside the cab. My stomach began to cramp and my head felt light. I leaned back and I felt David Ramirez's large hand ease me forward. He told me to put my head between my knees. I thought he was being unexpectedly considerate until I realized that he probably didn't want blood on his upholstery.

"I can't believe I almost hired you," he murmured. I heard the ticking of the turn signal. He kept talking to himself as the road became bumpy beneath the cushy suspension of his truck. "I'll take you home. My Alicia can fix you up."

In fifteen minutes the truck stopped and Ramirez opened the door for me. I saw a tidy yard and an old Pacific Northwest farmhouse sitting in front of a grassy field. The house was sided in painted cedar shakes. The front porch, set back under the second story of the building, had a hanging bench. The house was a moss green and looked as natural in its place as one of the old stumps that sat in the far corner of the field. A woman stood behind the screen door for a few moments, but when she saw her husband take me by the arm to help me out of the truck she came off the porch without asking questions.

Alicia Ramirez never asked a thing while she leaned me over the sink and washed my hair. I grimaced as she took a straight razor and cut the hair away from the cut. She had a light touch but the swelling around the cut was sensitive. Alicia was a very strong woman and, although gentle, she was not tentative. I believe she had experience in patching men back together. As she shaved the last section of hair, I gripped the porcelain sink and sucked my breath in. "*Lo siento.* Sorry," she said softly, but then worked the razor one last time.

She put butterfly bandages on the cut and light gauze around the area she had shaved. Finally she sat me down and gestured for me to take off my jacket. Her face grimaced as I slipped the jacket off and she immediately placed it out on the porch. David Ramirez handed me an ice pack.

"*Qué es eso?*" Alicia Ramirez asked her husband, pointing to my head.

"Simon Delaney," her husband answered, shaking his head as if trying to dismiss the foolishness of the entire world.

"So you're the great detective my husband tells me about." Mrs. Ramirez spoke in lightly accented English. She smiled and her dark eyes were bright under her curly hair.

"Yes," I said. "I am the great detective." And I put my hand gingerly on the bandage. "Thank you for taking care of my cut." She bowed in response.

"My daughter," she said, "my Angela, is buried in your town. That is as it should be, if that is where her children are to be. But I worry. I worry about where my grandchildren are. Do you know?"

"I saw them eating ice cream at my house just . . . I don't know . . . a day ago. They are staying with a very nice family down the street. They looked happy."

Alicia Ramirez nodded and said nothing. My cheap words of reassurance hung in the air between us.

David Ramirez walked over to a cabinet beside the back door. The cabinet was topped with cracked red linoleum but like everything in the house I had seen it was clean and sturdy. David Ramirez took a pistol in a leather holster off the top shelf. Then he took a box of shells.

"This girl of ours, Mr. Younger . . . ," he said as he started to load the revolver, "she was smart, and she loved animals and land. You've heard of the Future Farmers of America?"

I nodded my head that I had.

"Angela could have had a scholarship to go to agricultural school. She could have run livestock and raised feed. I had worked hard for her and had almost leased a section of land near the river bottom so she could have started her own place. But that was not what her . . . her new husband wanted."

Alicia tapped me lightly on the shoulder and spoke softly, "Simon did not approve of David. He didn't like the money David made."

"No," Ramirez said and shook his head grimly. "Simon Delaney does not like my money. Simon Delaney likes freedom." Ramirez looked at me as if he had more to say than he had words for. "But in this country people like me can still make money. And freedom *costs* money."

Ramirez flipped the breech shut and spun the cylinder. "That's all there is to it," he said and inspected the gun. The cylinder rolled easily several times. Ramirez gripped it in his right hand. Then he sat down on a kitchen chair. In his hand, the large-bore gun looked like a derringer. He leaned forward to me, and his expression was focused yet smoldering with anger.

"I know Communists. They are liars. They never give anybody what they want. They keep it for themselves."

David Ramirez stood up and unfolded the shoulder holster and put it on as if he were putting on a suit coat.

"I was going to give my daughter land. Simon Delaney gave her nothing. Angela lived in a trailer out in someone's driveway." He put on his canvas work coat, covering up the pistol. He looked at me for half a moment, and in that moment I had a flash of fear he was going to reach for the gun.

"You're going to need another coat," he said finally. "Go upstairs and look in the storage closet. There should be something for you there. Then we are going out to find Mr. Delaney."

The steps groaned and gave way as I climbed them. There were two doors at the top of the landing. A bare bulb hung from the ceiling. I tried the door on my right. Inside, the air was stale with dust and the faint odor of mold. I turned on the light and recognized the undisturbed melancholy of a dead girl's room. There was a single twin bed with a fitted pink bedspread, the pillow tucked in at the head. The bed had acorn carved posts and clawed feet. Next to it was a dressing table and a chest of drawers. Shelves held a few keepsakes: glass figurines of horses, a ballet dancer. There was a geometry textbook, a plastic vaquero on a black stallion, and dolls made from socks propped in the corner. A blanket was pinned on one wall under a poster from the movie about Richie Valens: a dark-haired boy with a cheap guitar slung over his back. Above the table, blue ribbons were tacked to a corkboard: Best in Show. On the table was a silver comb and a framed picture of a young woman holding a baby cradled in her arms. In the corner of the picture a man with a crooked grin peeked over her shoulder and smoked a cigarette.

Dusty lace curtains were tied back. Through the window I could see the yard; trimmed grass ran to the edge of an undeveloped field. I looked down on four strands of a clothesline with the wooden pins scattered on the wires like sparrows. Out in the field a man was working on a tractor in the rain.

The floorboards creaked behind me. Mrs. Ramirez blanched as she looked in the room. She was wiping her hands with a dish towel as her eyes rested on the photograph on the dressing table.

"That was her with her first. Her first husband. She took our family name after that. She never took Simon's." Mrs. Ramirez sighed, straightened her stance, and started to say something more: perhaps words to summarize, or to close, her daughter's life, but she didn't. She finished wiping her hands, then turned and walked away.

On the dimly lit landing she handed me a frayed canvas jacket that had been patched on the elbows. As she handed it to me, her fingers bit into my arm.

"Don't let him shoot Simon," Alicia Ramirez whispered, and her voice was urgent. "Killing Simon won't help. It won't bring our Angela back."

"I'll try, Mrs. Ramirez. But truthfully I'm not such a great detective." I told her this thinking that she was not a good woman to lie to.

She looked at me. Her eyes were sad but undefeated. "You have strength you haven't used," she told me.

I looked down at my wet shoes, not able to meet her eyes. "I don't know if that's true," I answered.

"Well, I do," she said and slipped my arm into the jacket, patting my back as I walked down the stairs.

As David Ramirez and I pulled out onto the paved road near his house, a police car hit its lights and pulled us over. Ramirez looked quizzically into the rearview mirror and unconsciously clamped his left elbow down against the pistol in his coat. He scowled at me as the police officer walked around the front of his car and over to the passenger side. I rolled down the window and the cop trustingly tucked his head down to my eye level.

"Hello, Dave." The neatly trimmed young cop had the hint of a drawl that creeps into some Washingtonians' speech. David Ramirez smiled weakly, nodded, then blurted out, "Hey, Chuck, what's the problem?"

The cop pushed his cap back with his index finger. "Aw, no problem really. We had a kid get beat up pretty bad last night. Bunch of guys gave him a blanket party, I guess. He was coming out of the bar playing pool and they bagged him. Roughed him up pretty good, left him in a ditch out toward the steam plant. We think it might be some Mexican kids. I was just wondering if you heard anything. I know you were out late. I mean, the last shift just had a note in their report that you were out late. You know, not that we suspect you or anything . . ."

"No," David Ramirez interjected nervously.

"No. We heard the boy was in the bar playing some pool and got into a scrape with some Mexican fellas."

This young cop clearly wasn't as dumb as he was acting. From the way he stopped us and from the way he came to the passenger side, he had a description of me already and was trolling for my reaction. My silence at this point could be taken as an admission of guilt. So I was about to break the cardinal rule of my profession and offer information to the police.

"Hey, I think I was in the bar when that happened!"

"The heck you say? Last night, down at the pool hall?" The cop spoke to me as his eyes were scanning every inch of the inside of the vehicle for anything that might be in "plain view" which would allow him to order me out of the car if he wanted. No, this was not some friendly interview.

"Yeah, some guy was playing pool with his girlfriend. Kind of a handsome kid, cowboy boots, T-shirt?"

"That sounds like it." The cop pulled out his notebook, then unclipped his mechanical pencil from his coat pocket. "Wow. I'm glad I ran into you. What's your name? Just so I can put it down in my report. They never believe I found a witness if I don't put down a name."

I gave him my name and all the numbers he could stand. I made up my Social Security number, not out of any mischief, but because I have been making up my Social Security number for six years now, ever since a kid robbed my locker at the swimming pool. I know this isn't a great idea, but so far I haven't had any fallout from it.

"How would you characterize this argument, the one in the pool hall?" the young cop asked me earnestly.

"It wasn't an argument really. I think it was mostly good-natured. Just joking around."

The cop didn't write anything down. Mostly because this wasn't what he wanted to hear.

"But it was racial in nature," he suggested. A pleading tone was entering the officer's voice. "I mean, the Mexican boys were pretty mad, weren't they? The kid had insulted their race and they were angry, isn't that right?" He tried to rehabilitate me.

"Naw," I said breezily. "Naw, I think it was pretty good-natured. Yeah, I do remember some Hispanic people in the bar but they were playing pool and laughing. And there were some words, but I must have left before the action got started." I shrugged, which made my head throb.

The cop leaned his elbows on the edge of the open window. He looked down at his feet, shaking his head.

"Okay. Listen . . ." he said to his shoes. "Would you mind coming with me for a few minutes, Mr. Younger? I want to take you to a place and have a look at a couple of guys. See if you can pick out some of the men you saw in the bar. It'll just take a couple of minutes. Okay?" He opened the car door and gestured toward his squad car in a way that suggested my voluntary cooperation wasn't voluntary.

I watched my own feet walking to the police car. The

cop was assuring David Ramirez that he would take me wherever I needed to go. I sat in the backseat of the squad car out of habit. I even held my wrists together until I realized I wasn't going to be cuffed. I knew I wasn't guilty of anything, but that didn't keep me from acting like a guilty man pretending to be innocent.

The cop spoke on the radio as he turned onto the main street of Centralia, back near the railroad tracks and across from Seminary Hill. We slowed as we approached a warehouse with an open delivery door. A pickup truck was parked there; nearby, some dark-haired men in work clothes were talking to a white man who looked to be a dispatcher of some type. There was another police car parked just around the corner to the north.

"Okay," the young cop spoke up, watching me in the rearview mirror, "just take a look at these guys. Why don't you get out of the car and walk over to the officer and ask him if he needs to talk to you. He knows you're coming and he won't ask you any questions. Just see if you recognize anyone."

We stopped and the Mexican men in work clothes standing at the pickup stared at us. Behind them the door of the other police car opened and the white boy got out. His eyes were nearly swollen shut. It appeared his cheeks were stuffed with gauze. His pretty cowboy boots were scuffed. I saw someone seated in the police car pointing at me.

As I walked up to the group of men, the old man and his son stared at me, but only briefly. The old man looked away, but the son's eyes burned into mine, without expression, but long enough to carry some intention, neither friendly nor threatening, almost beseeching . . . but angry.

I walked up to the cop who was talking amiably with the dispatcher and asked him if he needed to talk to me. He smiled broadly and answered in a whisper which revealed he had no dramatical talent, "No, I think we have enough from you. Thanks for coming down." He put his hand on my shoulder and as I turned back toward the street I didn't look at the men by the truck and I didn't look at the pretty boy who had had his face broken last night.

The police hadn't taken me in for a formal lineup but were satisfied with this clumsy show. But I had to do something. The pretty boy was talking to someone who remained seated in the distant car. My shepherd was still standing by his cruiser, smiling. I knew the cops had wanted to make it look as if I had already snitched off the Mexicans, which would not be healthy for me come nightfall, particularly since I knew the cops didn't have enough to make an arrest. If they had anything more than these cheap theatrics we'd all have been locked up by now.

The cop opened the back door for me and said, "Well, how'd you do?"

I stopped walking toward him. "Not so well," I said, then turned back around to the men by the truck and in a voice loud enough for everyone in the block to hear I said, "You know, all those people look alike to me. Hell, I don't know, I couldn't say if any of those guys were there last night."

The old man was still looking at his hands but his son threw a tool belt in the back of the truck and looked at me with a twisted grin. I turned back around to face my driver. The young cop frowned and signaled to me with his index finger.

"Okay, wise guy, get in the car."

I held my wrists out in front of me. "All right, O'Malley. Just as soon as you put me in custody."

He stepped back, confused. "I can't arrest you," he blurted out, "and my name's not O'Malley." He scratched his scalp under his hat.

"Oh," I said in my stage voice. "Well . . . I guess I'll

just be on my way then." I walked toward the back walls of the brick buildings that fronted Trower Avenue.

"But—" I heard him sputter, "I need a local contact for you."

I waved to him gaily over my shoulder. "I'll get a hold of you if I need to," I called and I hopped up on the curb near the train depot.

I was two blocks from the pool hall. A blue sky showed through the dark clouds. The wind seemed fresh in my face, with the hint of the fertile fields beyond town. There is nothing like walking away from an angry and sputtering police officer to give me a fresh outlook.

The first thing I noticed when I turned the corner onto Trower Avenue was that the door to the pool hall was wide open. Marcus was peering out from the eave that covered the cigar stand. When he saw me he turned instantly and walked inside. I hurried my step.

In the pool hall, Toddy was sitting with an old woman. She had both her hands in his. Her hair was pulled back in a tight white bun. Her skin was a mottled brown; great folds of wrinkles creased around her eyes, her chin. Her eyes focused on their hands resting on the oak table.

Toddy looked up at me and he smiled. "I stayed put," he said.

"I can see that. I'm sorry I didn't come back for you right away." I rubbed the back of my head. "I had a problem. Are you okay?"

Toddy smiled weakly and didn't let go of the old woman's hands. "Yeah. Mrs. Lee let me sleep downstairs in the basement. She said that it was a good place to let things blow over." Then he looked up at me quizzically. "Cecil, what does that mean exactly, 'blow over'?"

I sat down next to them. "It just means that you stay safe while trouble goes on around you. Like going inside when there is a storm going on. You did the right thing."

I turned to the old woman. "Thank you. Thank you for looking after him."

She nodded and now that she lifted her eyes I could see they were wet with tears. "There was a lot of trouble here last night," she said in a low voice. "I let him stay down in the basement. Many men have stayed in that basement when trouble blew through. You know?"

She paused and let go of Toddy's hands. She took a deep breath. "I'm Mary Lee. They've always called me China Mary. I'm Simon's grandmother."

I glanced around the gloom of the unlit bar. "Is Simon here?"

Mrs. Lee nodded toward the door to the side of the bar and a tear cupped in the deep fold under her left eye. Her lip trembled.

"That boy's grandpa never married me. He said he was going to but he didn't. That night they hung Wesley. This town was going crazy. They would have been hung for sure. They never did come back. Those boys."

Marcus emerged through the door. He stared at me with a dark seriousness that made my stomach hurt almost more than my head did. Mrs. Lee leaned forward and took Toddy's hand again.

"I had a girl. Irene. Her father was a Swede. She worked here, married that Irishman, Angus Delaney, they moved away. Later they came back with the baby." Here she nodded to the doorway where Marcus stood with his arms folded, scowling down at the floor. He too was breathing heavily.

She continued, "Angus died of the drink. He talked and he talked about Ireland . . . about bombs . . . he even talked about radical Indians hereabouts. But mostly he drank. After he died, my Irene was killed in a car wreck. That boy, that Simon read every book in the library." Here she stopped and could not go on. I looked at Toddy.

"They haven't called the ambulance," he whispered to me. "I think they should call the ambulance, Cecil." He was nodding toward the door near Marcus.

Then Mrs. Lee whispered, "That little boy could read comic books before he went to school. Simon knew more words than any of them."

I went to Marcus and started through the door, but his hand held me back. "Don't go down there, man," he said.

"Call an ambulance," I shot back, and Marcus shook his head sadly. But he let me go through the door.

The stairs were narrow slats down into a stone basement. Naked bulbs hung from the floor joists above. Pinball machines teetered in corners and rows of the old theater seats were wrapped in brown paper and folded against the walls. Paint cans with cracked and spattered labels were stacked in one corner alongside wooden barrels covered in dust. Under the stairs was the cot where Todd must have slept and around to the back was a door, behind which a furnace rumbled. There were beer signs from every era: An old-style bathing beauty and a portrait of Custer's Last Stand. Next to the furnace room door stood a stainless steel deep fryer pitched on its side. I pushed the furnace door open and walked into Simon Delaney's legs dangling down in the doorway.

A huge hand gripped my right shoulder. I turned and Marcus handed me a piece of yellow legal paper. "He left this. I suppose he wanted you to see it" was all he said.

The note was six lines in neat script. *Listen. I shot Angela. She said she was going to kill herself. I was going to stop her. I had been drinking, too. I took old Flynn's gun for protection. I thought. I killed her. She was going to shoot me. I wish to Christ she had. The old man can have his money back. Somebody try and do some good for those kids. There is nothing more to say.*

I flicked on the light. Simon Delaney's head was twisted at an impossible angle. His neck was almost cut by what looked like a wire rope awkwardly wrapped around the pipes in the ceiling. Stacks of boxes were scattered around the room as if he had kicked a good while before he died. He had almost bitten through his tongue. His eyes were open.

"He's dead." I said it out loud, turning quickly away from the body. "We'll have to cut him down." I was dizzy, trying not to get sick, as if I had a whole lifetime of stupidity boiling around in my stomach.

But there was something keeping me upright, like a stiffening in my shoulders and chest. I recognized that I was angry and feeling ripped off.

"Now where's the money?" I yelled up through the floor. "Where's Ole Hanson?"

Chapter Ten

Marcus's and my footfalls on the creaking stairs of that basement made me feel as if I were going to climb stairs for the rest of my life.

Just as we reached the doorway at the top of the stairs I heard the door rack against its frame. We walked through the door and stepped into the muzzle of David Ramirez's revolver.

"I know you are hiding him." The gun was shaking at the end of his arm, and David Ramirez's voice was cracking and uncertain.

"I am hiding him no longer," Marcus said calmly and he folded his arms across his chest.

Ramirez raised the revolver to the level of Marcus's eyes and clicked the hammer back. Todd helped Mrs. Lee to stand and they walked toward the door. I tried to ease around Marcus but his bulk blocked my way. I stared under his arm at David Ramirez as he cried.

"She would have been rich in this life. Here. With her mother and me. Now she is gone. You take me to him."

"You cannot kill him, Mr. Ramirez. But you can kill me if you like," Marcus said softly, and he stood taller, as if expecting the blow of lead into his skull. "But it will do you no good. You will be a killer, too. Your wife will live alone while you die in prison, and . . ." Marcus slowly reached out and put his fingers around the revolver in the older man's hand, "those children will have no grandpa."

Ramirez winced sharply, trying to pull the trigger. Imagining the drop and the kick. Imagining the smoke and blood spatter, the thud of the big man's body. But finally a sadness swept over his face and he dropped his arm. He uncocked the revolver. Marcus took the gun from him. He said quietly, "He's downstairs." Then he stepped aside.

Ramirez looked puzzled but walked past us down the stairs. Toddy and Mrs. Lee came back through the door from the street. Milky sunlight from the street spattered tiny rainbow patterns that moved across the dark oak wall.

Marcus reached into a drawer under the bar. He pulled out William Flynn's money tin and put it on the bar. When he opened it, I saw that it was now only half full of the old bills.

"I gave half to Mrs. Lee. You can take the rest back up to Mr. Flynn." Marcus nodded toward the basement door.

I had a foolish idea I should frisk Marcus, and in fact took a step toward him when the old woman spoke.

"Ole Hanson was Simon's grandpa," Mrs. Lee said softly. "Ole Hanson left the night of the lynching and I never saw him again. Simon said he lived in Alaska. I don't know." The old woman swayed. Todd helped her settle into a straight-backed chair. "Some years ago, Simon brought an old man here. They say he was Ole, my daughter's father. I don't know. He was just an old man. Sick. He was not happy. He didn't live long. Simon buried him near Wesley Everest. It never mattered to me. That old man. He was gone so long. I think it was more important to Simon. His own father had been such a disappointment to him. Simon thought that Ole must have been a . . . what?" She turned to Marcus, her head unsteady, her gaze dreamy and confused. "What would you call him?" she asked.

"A revolutionary hero," Marcus muttered, not meeting the old woman's gaze.

Mrs. Lee snorted a rueful laugh. "Ole Hanson was a foolish man. But he was handsome and he was full of fun." She tried to stand. "I'll show you," she said. "I'll tell you where."

Todd helped her up. I grabbed our gear, which was stacked in one of the bar chairs. As we walked out onto the street, I heard the percussive bang of a large-caliber pistol down in the basement. I looked up at Marcus. We kept walking.

The graveyard lay across the highway and out past the factory outlet stores. We had all loaded up in Marcus's white van and Marcus drove slowly. Mrs. Lee gripped the sides of the bucket seat in front as if she were about to fall out of the van at every bump. The road hummed with cars on pavement. Lighted signs flashed in broad daylight. A stereo system thumped in a truck beside us. The road was like an endless metallic Chinese lion, each dancer holding up a car and dancing down the paved river bottom.

There was a chain across the drive that led into the cemetery plots. This was a field with markers in an industrial district near a railroad spur. Hardly pastoral or parklike. More like a storage area for the dead. We walked down into the field and there, set back from the road, was the marker reading IN MEMORY OF WESLEY EVEREST: *Killed November 11, 1919. Age 32.* On the left-hand corner of the marker, the symbol of the IWW had been chipped away by the mower.

"That's that one," the old woman chirped comfortably as she walked by. Her thin fingers pointed without looking, as if these gravestones were familiar knickknacks.

"Here he is." Mrs. Lee stopped and she was leaning into Todd, gripping his arm with both hands. She was winded from the walk.

This stone read, OLE HANSON. BORN 1899. DIED 1987. *A hero to all who knew him.*

"I missed him bad at first. I was going to have a baby but I had to keep working. I was so romantic and such. I used to put flowers on Wesley's grave. Wanting to remember. I thought he was alive. They made me look at that body they found over by Oakville but it weren't him. Never. I said it was, though. I thought they'd stop looking for him."

She stared down at the stone. "I suppose they never found him." A red-winged blackbird flitted to the low branches of a fir tree.

"He never came back, though." The old woman spoke to no one in particular. We said nothing.

"I never married." She did not look up. Her voice was tinged with bitterness. "I had to keep working. I guess he just went fishing up there."

She squinted so her eyes completely disappeared behind the folds of eyebrow and cheek. I realized that in the bright sunlight she was nearly blind. She must have found her way through the graveyard by feel. Her head wobbled and she shaded her eyes, trying to pick me out.

"Simon read every book in the library, I think. He was my grandson. But he was all mine. He was never his father's."

Marcus walked away and sat down next to the grave of Wesley Everest. He rolled stones in his right hand.

Todd helped Mrs. Lee sit in the dry grass. She swept the gingham material of her dress under her legs.

"Simon told me I was a slave. He might have been

right. I worked real hard." The blackbird took to the air from the limb.

"Having Irene, having my grandson Simon made me happy. I had no complaints. Maybe I should have . . . But now everyone's dead." She shook her head and smiled at the bitterness of this joke.

The blackbird perched on the headstone across from us. His epaulets flashed red. The bird was ruffled and agitated.

"You came down from Alaska?" Mrs. Lee asked me.

"Yes," I said, probably too loud.

"You take him back." She nodded to Ole Hanson's stone. "You take him back. He was never mine."

The blackbird cackled, turned on the branch, and flew away. I tried to follow his path but he was gone now.

Chapter Eleven

"You have to appreciate my situation, young fella." William Flynn settled himself on the stump near the overrun garden in front of his homestead. "I *had* to act dingy in the head. Hell, that boy was going to frame me up for killing Angela. How the hell did I know I was going to get off? I couldn't trust the damn lawyer."

I looked up at the old man from the bottom of the hole I was digging and didn't speak.

"Simon had been to my room," William went on. "He took that old gun and was headed over to get Angela. He said she was out of her mind. They'd been drinking. I knew it was trouble. I wasn't about to call the damn cops. I tried to stop it. I made it to the bottom of the stairs in the hotel when I heard the shot. I stopped right there. Simon came barreling down the stairs and he beat me back to my room. The gun was there when the police came later. What the hell was I going to tell them?"

I was finishing up digging the grave that was to lie between the cabin and the root cellar. "Why not just tell the truth? Help the cops catch Simon?" I asked him without turning away from the digging.

"Hell, son, Simon Delaney knew where Tommy was."

"You mean Ole Hanson," I sputtered and threw another wet shovelful.

"Whatever," the old man said. "Simon knew where my partner was buried. Do you think he'd a ever told me where if I turned him in to the damn cops for shooting Angela? No, sirree. He would have just snitched me off to them cops. My way, I got you to do my finding out for me. Simon was a damn rummy. I knew if you found him you'd get the truth somehow. Hell, son, I knew what I was doing. Even if it had gone bad. They would have just put me in some other damn hospital. They never would have put a crazy old coot like me in prison. No, sir."

I stopped shoveling and stared down into the grave, winded. Simon Delaney was dead. William Flynn wasn't all that crazy or senile and all the rest of the living had managed to get a year older. And now it was Todd's birthday again and we were gathered up at the Flynns' cabin to rebury an old man who had spent the first years of the twentieth century as Ole Hanson and the rest of it as Tommy Flynn.

Having a body legally exhumed and transported by ship turned out to be complicated and irritating. Thank God for Pirate Ron and Bob the Fisherman. Smuggling a moldering corpse in the hull of a fishing boat suited their particular views of the world. They were skeptical, but by the time I told them just part of the story, they were in. It had everything for them: danger, illegality, and weirdness.

Getting ahold of Ole Hanson had taken the perpetration of fraud, for to have a body exhumed in Washington, the body has to be turned over to a licensed entity who has the authority to transport and dispose of bodies. So we stole him. Ron the Pirate forged the papers in a messy hand and drove the delivery truck to the cemetery in Centralia. The cemetery keeper was a closet anarchist himself and as long as he was covered, he had no problem with the theft of one of his charges. "I'm sure he'll enjoy the trip," he said cryptically as Ron loaded Ole's coffin into the back of a panel van. Ron drove the coffin up the coast to Bellingham where he had moored his troller. The coffin wouldn't fit in the hold of the old wooden boat, so Ron had to lay Ole out on the ice blanket in the hold.

"It wasn't so bad as you'd think," Ron told me later. "That old boy was all dried out nice, light as a feather really, and he was sewn up in a cheesecloth sort of thing so I didn't have to worry about losing any parts off him or anything."

Now David Ramirez took the shovel out of my hand and offered to spell me on the grave digging. He had come to Sitka to move the rest of his grandchildren's stuff home to Centralia and he offered to help bury the old man. The Centralia Police Department had been concerned at first when they saw the bullet wound in Simon Delaney's hanging body. But even the most junior of them could make out the wound was postmortem. David Ramirez had put a bullet in his son-in-law as he hung from the pipes. The police seemed to understand that a vengeful man with a gun almost has to shoot someone. It's like a law of nature or something. The DA made some talk about charging Ramirez with tampering with a corpse or unlawful discharge of a weapon. But the police just took a statement from him and let the whole mess go.

I carried Tommy Flynn's body off the deck of the fishing boat. We had all agreed that once the corpse entered Alaskan waters he would be referred to as Tommy. Ole Hanson had died and been buried in Centralia, Washington ten years ago. I lifted the cheesecloth bundle and teetered down the narrow planking that was the makeshift dock at the Flynns' anchorage. The body was light and rigid. Although

I tried not to breathe through my nose. When I did I picked up only a light chemical smell. I was mostly struck by how cold the body felt. The fires were all out. Tommy Flynn was more still than a sleeping child, more still, even, than a stone.

I placed him in a yellow cedar box that lay open near the stump where William Flynn was sitting. Bob the Fisherman had carved a memorial to William's exact specifications. It read: *Tom Flynn also known by his birth name, Arnold "Ole" Hanson. A fine man who mostly tried to do good.* Underneath the block lettering was carved a cormorant sitting on a rock drying its wings, its long neck arched high and holding the symbol of the Industrial Workers of the World.

David Ramirez stopped digging. He was well below the level of the garden. His head was down in the hole. He used the ends of roots to help claw his way out of the hole.

"Deep enough," he said and wiped his hands on his pants.

Jane Marie, Young Bob, and Todd were in the cabin cooking up Todd's birthday meal. Jane Marie had spent the morning cleaning the wild strawberries we had picked in Gustavus and had saved in our new freezer. While she had done that I cleaned the cabin and put up balloons and a banner in the rafters.

Angela's children were looking wide-eyed at the cedar coffin. Thomas had been down on the tide flat all morning. His pants were wet all the way through. He had black sand smeared down his nose. The children walked over to William Flynn, tugging on his fingers. Then the boy pointed to the coffin and asked, "William, is that your brother?"

William stayed on the stump and leaned over on his cane. "No," William Flynn said. "Not really."

"Well, who is it?" the boy asked.

William didn't say a thing for a while. Down on the beach the tiny rock crabs were scuttling back to the rocks the boy had tipped. The light dappled off the water and the warm breeze carried the sound of breaking surf in from the mouth of the anchorage.

William picked a twig off the stump and pointed to the box that was only a couple of feet away. "That there? That's my partner. His body, really. It's what he left behind." William squinted at the dark-eyed boy, who looked so much like his dead mother. "Like a track you leave in the sand, you know?"

The boy shook his head and said nothing. Finally his sister punched him on the shoulder and said, "He's up in heaven like Momma, dope. Let's go back to the beach." And she ran off, cantering like a loose-limbed colt, her black braids streaming behind her. The boy lingered for a moment, then he gave William a quick hug and lunged after his sister.

William Flynn didn't take his eyes off the two children playing on the beach. Then he took a deep breath. "I used to run like that. Long time ago." In the distance I could hear the surf breaking on the rocks. A raven dropped a clamshell on the beach, cracking it open. The old man's voice sailed out away from the closed coffin and into the distance.

"My name was Harvey Sparks back then. Used to play around like that in my mama's garden. You see her picture in my stuff?"

I nodded, squatting on the ground near him while I started to clean my dirty fingernails with the point of my jackknife blade.

William said, "I got older and started to ride the rails to the wheat harvests all through the West. You had to have a Red card if you rode on the rails back then. The Reds were almost as tough as the Bulls. A fella didn't really have much of a choice. I got to making speeches, up around Everett and west of Seattle. If a boy got hurt out in the woods the bull-buck used to just have him thrown up on a stump and take him in at the end of the day. Hell, men were treated no better than the animals. I truly do believe it was worse than slavery. Man had no choice and no one to look out for him. I did my first free speech fight in Montana. We plugged the jails with hoboes from all over the territory until they had to start letting us go. I talked up in Everett right before they shot up the docks."

The herring had come into the cove and the eagles had perched in the tall spruce trees. An eagle carved the air down to the beach for a fish. The limb kept bobbing as William spoke.

"After the mess in Centralia we needed new names. My father was William. That's his picture in the trunk, too. He died of influenza back when I was in Montana, so I took that name. Tommy didn't care much what he was called. He wanted to be named Joe Hill, but I thought that was too damn silly and would attract attention. Tommy was like that. He had a swagger. All our lives he kept that. He was different from me and maybe that was why I didn't want to let him out of my sight."

William pushed against his cane and stood up from the stump, took two unstable steps, and sat down on the lid of Tommy's coffin. He pressed the flat of his hand against the fragrant yellow wood. He silently traced the inscribed lettering of the name, while across the harbor lazy swells broke over the shallow rocks.

The voices of the children came up from the beach and William turned his head but his attention was far off. "I went to Centralia to listen to the speech one of the members was going to give. The committee had asked me to come. The hall was crowded. That Britt Smith gave me a sandwich, and after the main speaker I got up on the soapbox and gave 'em what-have-you. I used some damn fine language on them. Those boys were all stirred up like a bunch of hornets and I thought I must have really done a good job with the talking, but then they told me they were getting their guns together to defend the hall. I told them it was goddamn foolish and it wasn't going to work. But maybe we were all crazy from the start.

"Later they said that boy up on the hill was crazy, but he weren't crazy to start with, that I ever knew of, anyway. He might have been scared crazy that night. I wouldn't doubt that. That boy, they called him 'Grand Mound.' Hell, he was plunking away with a twenty-two high-power. I don't think he never hit anybody but with what felt like a bee sting. It must have been a thousand yards down that hill to the hall. Hell of a long shot. Couldn't see hardly anything.

"I told them I wasn't going to go along with any of it. Defending that hall against those soldiers was pure foolishness. We weren't going to win that fight. What the hell did they think was going to happen? We could have pulled in more members. Put on a strike. Plug the jails. Make more of a point, not just start killing fellas. What? We were going to shoot some of them Legion boys and then everybody'd just say, 'Well, all right then, it was self-defense.' That's nuts, and that goddamn lawyer should have known that, too. I told Tommy. I told him right there at the hall. He just said, 'Are you a sissy? For all your talk, what do you believe? You act like a damn scissor-bill.' I said, 'Hell, no. I'm for the One Big Union more than any man, but what the hell you think's going to happen after all this shooting?' And Tommy gets his trunk. He puts his two-fifty Savage in it, and that Grand Mound kid puts the twenty-two there, and they lock the trunk away by the door. The kid says, 'We got a right to defend our property just like any white man.'

"Tommy told me he had a cabin up the Hannaford River. I told him we'd all better get out of town quick no matter what happens and he said if I want to go I could go but he was going up on the hill and defend the hall with the others. I walked up there with them. Curly was scared bad. He had his thirty-two-twenty and he kept cocking it and uncocking it. The parade went by. Christ, you could hardly see anything. They moved down the hill, tried to get a closer look. Curly kept saying, 'I hope to hell nothing happens.' I told him to just come on, he didn't have to do anything. But Tommy shushed me up. You know he had been a boxer? He loved to fight. He was good with a gun, a terrific shot. He didn't go in the war or anything. I think that was some of it. Tommy was tired of listening to those soldiers brag about the war. He used to say, 'Shit, all the damn heroes. They couldn't hit a cow from inside her belly.'

"Well, the parade came back around and I still, to this day, don't really know what happened. I remember the Legion boys were milling around in front of the hall. I remember Curly Bland muttering, 'Goddamnit.' There were Legion boys running toward the hall. It was such a long way, the sound was funny. There were popping sounds for sure, but I don't know if it was shooting or the windows breaking. But three of them up on the hill started shooting. I don't know. They must of each shot twenty or thirty times toward the crowd. Curly and Grand Mound, they were just shooting wild. But I could see Tommy aim and squeeze, aim and squeeze. They could have killed some of those boys. I don't know, but I never saw where anything hit. I don't know who started it at all. I was there and I still can't tell you. It wasn't their fault I don't think. They were scared. They wanted to help the boys inside the hall.

"Some of the Legion boys were breaking into the hall and everybody else was scattering around. Some people were screaming, but like I say, sounds came up on the hill so slow it was dreamy, you know, like we weren't really part of it. Then some of the Legion boys came running and shooting down the alley to the east and I could see them grouping up, then chasing down the alley. I heard more popping sounds and I

said we had better get the hell out of there because they were
going to lynch every last one of us.

"We tore off down the hill and the other boys had
their guns. Tommy kept his old thirty-eight pistol. The
blackberries cut into us bad. We rolled and fell down that
damn trail. We headed back down the hill to the east. Curly
and Grand Mound took off. They said they were going to
try and find some friends to hide them out. They took off
toward the river. Like I say, Tommy and I wanted to head up
the Hannaford River. He had that hunting cabin and I knew
there was some food up there. We hid in some old farmer's
shed for a while and I looked out at the fields and such, and
I told Tommy to say good-bye to it all 'cause we were never
going to be safe there again. He didn't say nothing but just
held on to his pistol, rubbing on the grips. He didn't say a
thing for a good long while. Then he just stood up and said
he had better go back and get that damn trunk he left up on
the hill. I told him it was crazy but he said he was going. He
just left and I followed him for a while. Everywhere people
were running around with guns. Some of them had axes and
such. I saw one man walking down Trower Avenue with a
chunk of rope. There was yelling and agitation, like a pack of
wild dogs running in that town. We worked our way around
to the south. There was lots of commotion near the river and
downtown, so we swung in a large circle until we ended up
on the other side of town under the railroad bridge. Some
of the hoboes had stocked canned food and tins of biscuits
back under the bridge. The Chehalis River ran there just below the fork of the Skookumchuck. The river was wide there
and pretty slow. We could swim it if we had to. Tommy and
I just hunkered there. He figured to wait till midnight or so
and then sneak back into town. He was going to see his girl
and go get that trunk. I tried to tell him there was no use in
that. They probably found that trunk and if they caught him
with his girl they'd likely kill her, too. He was doing Mary

Lee no favor going back. He said he didn't care but he didn't go back into town anyway, because they came right to our bridge.

"It was darker than the inside of a cow back under that bridge. So when we heard the trucks coming, we just ducked back in deeper, thinking they'd never see us. I heard them talking and swearing. I could hear them pulling something out onto the bridge just above our heads and I thought, 'My God, they're going to hang some poor fella' and just like that, right down in front of us, I could see a boy's body flailing all around. He was naked and white like a ghost almost. He was choking and arching his poor back. They never broke his neck that first time, but had used a poor rope to hang a man. The men who hung him were speaking softly to each other. It was so strange. They pulled the poor boy back up. Now someone shined the light of their truck out on the bridge. It was almost like a show. They dropped him again with a longer rope this time. It scared me bad. The poor devil was naked and all shiny. They broke his neck fine this time. He curled around and stopped moving except for swinging back and forth like an old parlor clock. Then they started shooting at him. The bullets tore into his body and spun him around and round, winding the rope up around his neck. Then he'd spin free the other way. Boys on the bridge speaking softly really, calling him a 'Red bastard.' I heard one of them call the dead man 'Mr. Smith.' I guess they thought he was Britt Smith who ran the Wobbly Hall, but it wasn't never Britt Smith they hung. It was that boy called Wesley Everest. I remembered him from the meeting. He was a cracker, that boy. Strong for the One Big Union and they killed him there that day with not so much as a thought about the law or what they were doing.

"They cut him down and he fell into the shallow part of the river. Tommy and I pulled way back in under the bridge because we thought they were going to come down the bank to go after that boy's body. But they didn't just then. They just got into their trucks and left. They didn't say much. Not much cussing or anything. It was the strangest thing.

"Tommy and I stayed under that bridge a good long while. We couldn't do a thing to help him. He was surely dead. There was no helping him. I'm sure of that. That boy was dead. People talk about how they cut the boy's privates off and how he died so slow. Well, I never saw that. I only heard about that later and I can't think. I looked at his broken neck; his head looking so big and pulled up and crooked with his tongue sticking through his teeth. I just know he was dead and we couldn't have helped him. Or stopped what happened.

"A good while after they left we scrambled out of there. We made it down south along the river and then we cut back up and made it finally to the Hannaford cabin, but we didn't stay there long. Everywhere we went there were men looking for Wobblies. Finally we found an old farmer who didn't ask us about our clothes or anything and he gave us a ride toward Tacoma. From there we rode a train up to Seattle. I think the old farmer knew we were lamming it, but he was mad at the Legion boys for running all over the country tearing up folks' farms and shooting up the ranches looking for Reds. You know, there were lots more people that liked the Wobblies than you'd think if you only read the newspapers. Hell, those newspapers were owned by businessmen. They couldn't tell the truth. I think the old ranchers and the folks out in the country knew the score. They had sons that got killed in the war and killed in the woods, and they still didn't really know what those sons died for. Those folks out in the country were pretty friendly to the Wobs. We got a meal or two. 'Course we didn't get up and give any speeches or anything.

"Tommy and me, we made it up to Seattle and found a Wob that was going to help us. He didn't ask any questions.

He didn't want to know our real names. We almost got on a clipper ship loaded with timber for Australia. But Tommy didn't want to go cause he didn't think they would speak enough English in Australia. I think he got it all mixed up with Austria. But whatever it was, Tommy said he wasn't going to go off to a place on the other side of the earth just for sticking up for what he believed. And anyway we couldn't get the papers we needed to get on that clipper ship. Finally, we made some arrangements for riding a steamer up to Alaska. We were supposed to go all the way up to Seward. We rode down in the coal bin and had to shovel for our passage. It was rough passage that winter. We was throwing up all the way to Alaska. Especially crossing Dixon Entrance. By the time we docked in Ketchikan we'd had enough. Tommy and I got off there.

"But like I said, we needed new names. I had seen the Rebel Girl give a speech in Seattle. She had been friends with Joe Hill. She had stirred up the workers all over the world. Her name was Elizabeth Gurley Flynn. I had always liked the name. I had liked the Irish fellas I knew in the movement so I took the name of Flynn. Tommy and me, we kept an eye on each other, so we became brothers. We were always together. It was easier to explain that way. Brothers."

William Flynn's voice was cracking and tired. He sat still except for his huge hand patting the lid of the coffin.

"They tried the rest of the Wobs for murder. They never touched those men that lynched poor Wesley. Tommy always said we should have gone back, said we should have stood trial with the rest of the boys. We could have told 'em our side. We could have helped."

William shook his head. "It was a bad idea to shoot those Legion boys like that. No matter what kind of bastards they were. After that we were no better than they were. We couldn't help anybody. Nothing we could have said would have helped anyone. When you start killing people, you got to get used to killing, and nothing anybody says matters anymore."

The grave was dug in the loamy ground. The dirt piled in mounds around the lip was red and gray with volcanic sediment. The sides of the trench were slick with moisture, and water was standing in the bottom of the hole even though it hadn't rained in a week. Ole's body had been in a crypt in Centralia but here in the soil of his garden in a few weeks he would be a part of the earth, part of the sea.

David Ramirez pounded the last nails into the lid. Then we lowered the coffin into the hole with some line from the fishing boat. The eagles and gulls wheeled high above the house, scouting the nearby coves. Three ravens sat on the ridge line of the cabin, knowing that food was being prepared inside.

Finally the children wandered up from the beach. The boy was riding on Todd's shoulder and the girl was swinging a whip of kelp. Jane Marie and Todd came out of the cabin, both of them wiping their hands on rags that were dusted with flour. Young Bob followed them out, carrying a wooden spoon covered in chocolate frosting. He had traces of icing striped down his chin. William Flynn sat on his stump looking down at the grave, neither sad nor angry. He looked tired and ready for rest.

Jane Marie knelt beside him, and gave the old man a hug. As the children came to the edge of the grave, they stopped and looked at this old man who was impossibly old to them, and they watched the cedar box carefully, for any sign of movement within.

William turned to the kids. "Oh, children . . . ," he said softly, "dead people have always frightened me so." He looked at the coffin, then back to the wide-eyed kids. "It's like they don't want to talk to us, these dead people. They don't *want* to hear how much we miss them. I could open up that box and scream in Tommy's ears and shake his damned old head on a rock but he will not listen. I could be the smartest talker in the world. I could stand on a stump and give a speech in any language that would change the world but still . . . he will not answer."

The children stared at him, unbelieving. "But do you know what I think?" he asked them. They silently shook their heads back and forth. "I think the dead cannot be convinced of anything. So we should not try."

"Or at least you shouldn't try and use big words." Todd spoke up from out of nowhere and we laughed.

William nodded in agreement like a stump speaker drawing in his crowd. He looked around at us: strange people headed toward an even stranger future. I could hear the eagles bickering above. A tiny bit of white down drifted from the trees and landed on the head of Angela Ramirez's son.

William hooked his fingers under his suspenders and clung to them. "There never was a perfect world," he said. "There was only death, and the language of happiness. People who tried to tell the truth and people who tried not to. I was both. My partner here was both. Tommy and I were the only ones we could talk to and we were happy a long, long time." William squinted up into the sun, his lips trembling. He struggled for something more to say but he failed.

Young Bob was sitting on the far end of the coffin tapping nervously on the lid with his prosthetic hook. He hadn't been there to see us carry Tommy up so I think he assumed the box was still empty. But maybe not. As William struggled for words Young Bob jerked the wooden spoon from his mouth and blurted out, "Hey, William, can we start the party yet?"

William Flynn squinted at the boy as if he were an exotic plant. "By God, that's a good idea," he said.

The children broke for the cabin. Bob the Fisherman brought his ice cream maker up from the boat along with some flaked ice from the fish hold. As I went into the cabin

Pirate Ron and David Ramirez started to cover the coffin with earth. This year, Toddy's birthday dinner was pancakes with berries and venison chops. William Flynn had given us enough of his money to make up all of the missing house payments. There was enough, too, to buy a new freezer. The venison chops and the berries had come from this freezer.

As I flipped the pancakes and listened to the racket of children blowing their paper horns, I thought about how much there was in this life I didn't deserve: both good and bad. And I almost felt guilty for buying a house and a new freezer with money I hadn't really earned. I also felt a little bad for cooking and not helping the other men in covering the coffin. But apparently I didn't feel bad enough to change what I was doing. I resolved to take them a plate of berries after they had filled in the grave. The berries were ripe and so sweet. Sweet enough, I thought, to compensate for anything.

Author's Afterword

In 1984, I had lost my job clearing trails for the Forest Service in Sitka and I needed someplace to have my morning coffee. I was trying to compile a book of oral histories of Alaskan pioneers, and I was starting to earn a buck as a criminal defense investigator for a young guy who had escaped Harvard Law to begin his frontier practice. This may sound unusual, but I think it is fairly typical for people who want to live on northern islands to be inventive when it comes to making a living.

That winter I ended up having tea with a resident from the Pioneers' Retirement Home named Bill Hills. Bill had been born in 1900. He and his brother had lived in a remote cabin for some thirty years, fishing a small trolling boat on the northern coast of the archipelago. One day, on our way down the street, we passed the American Legion Hall and Bill angrily spat on the lawn. I was shocked because Bill was ordinarily a mild-mannered and gentle man. When I asked about his reaction, all he would say was, "Legion boys hung a Wobbly down in Centralia." That is how these things start. This book is a result of my walk that day with Bill Hills.

Unfortunately, I'm a fiction writer and a private investigator so I have a slippery relationship to truth telling. But the more I learned about the events in Centralia, Washington, the more I wanted to write about the Armistice Day parade of 1919. To this day, many of those events are clouded in partisan controversy. Here is a sketch of the official record:

On November 11, 1919, during the first Armistice Day parade, three men were killed by gunfire when the parade stopped in front of the Industrial Workers of the World Hall. A fourth man, Ernest Dale Hubbard, was killed trying to capture Wesley Everest, who fled the scene and attempted to swim the Skookumchuck River. That night, Wesley Everest was taken from the Centralia jail by a contingent of citizens and lynched. No one was ever charged in the lynching, but eleven Wobblies were tried for first-degree murder, including Elmer Smith, the young attorney who had advised the IWW members that they could use force to defend the hall. Two of the Wobblies were acquitted, including lawyer Smith. Loren Roberts, the young man from Grand Mound who was the only member of the Wobblies to give a contemporaneous interview, was adjudged guilty but insane. The jury, clearly rattled by the intense passions surrounding the case, found the other nine guilty of "third-degree murder," which under the laws of Washington was a nonexistent charge, necessitating the court to change the convictions to second-degree. Two Wobblies were never captured: "John Doe" Davis and Ole Hanson.

In 1984, I indulged myself in a fantasy that Bill Hills and his brother were the two fugitives from Centralia. But this was not so. Although Bill Hills was a member of the IWW and did tell me the parable of the Japanese cormorant, neither he nor his brother was involved in the Centralia riot.

In my story, the events of the parade and the lynching are drawn from my reading of the historical record. The actions and motivations of Ole Hanson and Mr. Sparks, who were reported to be in the hall the night before the parade, were created out of my imagination as I walked the scene and reviewed the documents. Much is unresolved about the incident: Did the Legionnaires attack the hall *before* the shooting started? Although the record indicates that it is most likely that unarmed Legionnaires attacked the hall before shots were fired, it still sparks controversy among the partisans that stand in rank on both sides of this case up until this very day. Did someone in the lynch mob that night castrate Everest? The story has taken his mutilation into lore, but others insist there is no evidence for it.

My story doesn't try to tell the whole story or resolve the historical ambiguities of the incident. I was drawn to the case precisely *for* its ambiguity; I didn't try to tamper with it.

I was guided in my reconstruction by two fine books: *The Centralia Tragedy of 1919: Elmer Smith and the Wobblies*, by Tom Copeland, and *Wobbly War: The Centralia Story*, by John McClelland, Jr. To both authors I am indebted, particularly to Mr. McClelland for his generous loan of original materials and his advice along the way.

In Centralia, I am indebted to Margaret Langus, Margaret Shields, and Brenda O'Connor, of the Lewis County Historical Association, and John Baker of Stricklin Greenwood Cemetery. I owe a debt, too, to the many waitresses, clerks, cooks, and laborers I pestered for directions and impressions as I stomped around their community. From them I learned that Centralia is much more than the story of the riot.

In Dutch Harbor, I need to thank my friend and former colleague, Glen Herbts, for his kindness in showing me his fair city. My portrayal of the Chief of Police in Dutch Harbor is nothing like Glen Herbts, except for the eccentric laugh.

In Seattle, I'm indebted to Emmett Watson for his introduction to the dynamic personality of Susan O'Shea, who ministers to the street community on the waterfront of Seattle, and to John Caughlan and Jim Halpin who gave me background into the politics of the Pacific Northwest. I am grateful to Judge Michael Fox, who lent me books and gave me the benefit of his interest in the labor movement, and to my parents, Walter and Rachel Straley, who harbored me during my research trips.

It should be noted that any inaccuracies or failures of proper emphasis in my story are my fault and not due to the efforts of any of the people listed above.

My thanks also go to my friends in Sitka who lavish their patience on me: Nita Couchman and Marilyn Newman, for their quick reads and reality checks; the late Joe Scott (the gardener of Greentop), for his insights into the local plantings; and Pattiann Rogers of Colorado, for her correspondence and poetry. Finally, to Bill Hills: He is gone now and, although he is not a character in this book, my respect for him fills every page.